Nightsong

Nightsong

MARGARET E. KELCHNER

Beacon Hill Press of Kansas City

Kansas City, Missouri

ISBN 083-411-5298

Printed in the
United States of America

Cover design: Crandall Vail

Illustration: Keith Alexander

All Scripture quotations are from the King James Version of the Bible.

10 9   8   7   6   5   4   3   2   1

ABOUT THE AUTHOR

After writing many years primarily for Christian magazines, Margaret E. Kelchner has recently turned to writing Christian novels based on history. Her first novel, *Father of the Fatherless,* was released in 1993, followed in 1994 by *A Shadow from the Heat.*

Mrs. Kelchner makes a pointed effort to describe from firsthand observation the places portrayed in her novels. "I like to visit places I anticipate writing about," she explained in recounting her preparations for *Nightsong.* "I enjoy getting a feel for the whole atmosphere—the lay of the land, the sea, the rocks, what the undergrowth is like. I try to look beyond what is there today and see it in its more pristine setting as it may have been at the time of the story."

It was in the summer of 1992 that Mrs. Kelchner and her husband visited Castine, Maine, the setting of *Nightsong.* "We walked the streets there and read many historical markers throughout the town. We read the marker about the boy burned at the stake [an event upon which one incident in this novel is based] and talked with some of the people in the shops about the history of the area. I like to go back in my mind to what it might have been like if I had been a visitor in that era." Mrs. Kelchner noted that she based the Jarden home and its occupants in *Nightsong* on an actual dwelling in Castine, the home of a sea captain and his family.

Mrs. Kelchner and her husband, Raymond, spend their summers in Anderson, Indiana, and winters in Apache Junction, Arizona, near Phoenix at the foot of the Superstition Mountains. The couple has 3 children, 9 grandchildren, and 12 great-grandchildren.

"My greatest desire in writing these stories is that the people who read them see the golden thread of salvation throughout them," Mrs. Kelchner stresses. "I hope that many non-Christians will read my books, too, and will conclude about the Christian life, 'If it works for them [the characters], it may work for me.' I want all my readers to have the recognition that God is there—not *will be* there, but *is* there—in *their* times of trouble as well."

INTRODUCTION

To walk the quiet, tree-lined streets of Castine, Maine, past the remains of old Fort George—built by the British back in the 1700s to head off an expected invasion from the Continental forces—one is taken back to the days of the Revolutionary War, when courageous people of a fledgling nation sought freedom from tyranny.

Under the cruel occupation by the British, who saw the people as anarchists, disloyal to the crown, residents saw everything of value confiscated by the Redcoats: food, property, boats, and livestock. Sympathizers with the Revolutionaries and anyone suspected to be involved in counteraction were dealt with harshly.

Located on a small peninsula reaching into Penobscot Bay, Castine had a fine natural deepwater harbor suitable for tall ships. Settlers also took advantage of the proximity to some of the best timber available for shipbuilding. The French became the first settlers in the area, followed by seafaring people, farmers, and shipbuilders. Sea captains constructed elaborate homes there. Some of the finest, most durable, tall-masted ships plying the oceans were built in the Penobscot River area. The British were quick to recognize the importance of this natural seaport, sending ships and troops to establish a base of operation there.

Harsh Maine winters and the ever-present danger of Indian attack had strengthened the moral fiber of these hardy village people cut off from the help of Continental forces. One feeble attempt failed miserably because of indecision and fear.

Despite the cruel treatment they suffered at the hands of the occupying forces, along with many other hardships they were forced to endure, these strong-willed settlers of Castine held to their dream of independence and fought for the survival of the new nation in their own way.

History has recorded the national heroes from this struggle for independence, but until one walks the now-tranquil streets of this historic spot and reads the markers telling of the great sacrifice, he or she will not know of the unsung heroes who lived and died there. Many of the original buildings and homes are still there, preserved and cared for by the residents who live in them today.

Though a work of fiction, this story is based on historical fact discovered in the area. It is a written tribute to the courage and great spiritual strength demonstrated in the lives of these brave people who believed in a providential God.

1

ROSA SURGOSA JARDEN stood silently by her father's side, tears streaming down her face. It had been a hard and tragic voyage, and now, after months at sea, they were coming home at last.

Always she had been thrilled and excited as her father's three-masted cargo ship sailed into the Penobscot Bay to make its way between Isle au Haut and Deer Island into Castine Harbor. But today her heart was heavy. Even the Isle au Haut with its teeming life of wild birds held no interest for her. In the past, she had delighted in the funny antics of the puffin birds and mimicked their throaty "Hey, Al!" calls. This time they went unnoticed. Seals resting on a rocky ledge lazily reared their heads to watch the approach of her father's ship, but she paid them no heed as she strained her eyes to catch a glimpse of the familiar rise of ground that was home.

Home! What would it be like now, without her mother? she wondered, swallowing hard to keep down a sob that threatened to escape. She tried not to think about the barrel of rum down in the hold of the ship that preserved the body of her dear mother, who had died at sea, "until they could give her a proper burial," as her father had said. She glanced up at him, a handsome, robust man with graying black hair. His face, haggard and expressionless, was reddened by long years on the sea. Deep lines etched there told of the grief he unsuccessfully tried to conceal. The gray mist of the cold, blustery morning clung to his beard and dripped unnoticed from the brim of his hat. His hands were clenched tightly at his sides.

A large swell claimed her attention as it broke over the trim prow of the *Surgosa Rose,* sending an icy spray over them. It stung her cheeks, mingling with the tears. Her father's firm grasp steadied her as she pushed long strands of wet golden hair back beneath the hood of her dark, heavy cape.

"You had better go below," he said gently. "You might catch your death of cold."

In all her 16 years of life, Rosa had never disobeyed her father's wishes, but now she stood rooted to the spot. She shook her head, brown eyes appealing to him as she cried brokenly.

"I can't, Father. I mustn't. I wouldn't be able to bear it. Please let me stay!"

Captain Jarden only nodded his consent with eyes fixed on the distant harbor before him. The water was becoming more calm now as they rounded the long, rocky finger of land that marked the entrance to Castine Harbor. The crew set about hoisting the British flag and preparing for safe anchor.

"Cap'n, there's a strange ship off the port side," exclaimed Caleb Hummer, her father's first mate, pointing a bony finger in the direction of the boat half hidden by a small island. "It's not bearin' a flag."

Captain Jarden raised his telescope to peer through the mist at the strange vessel, a transport.

"Right you are, Caleb—what can it mean?" he replied, pondering over the discovery. Could the rumors he had heard about the colonies reclaiming some of their territories to the north be true? He lowered his glass and glanced at the scowling face of his first mate.

"It's not meanin' any good fer the British, sir—no siree— or it'd be bearin' colors," the old seaman replied, shaking his shaggy head.

Rosa stared wide-eyed at the ship in question as her father scrutinized it again. Giving a grunt, he remarked, "Caleb, there's no unusual signs to indicate it's a war ship. It appears peaceful enough. I can see no activity aboard that would lead me to suspicion otherwise."

Caleb pulled the stump of a pipe from his pocket and stuck it into his mouth. His narrowed gaze never left the craft as he studied it with the experienced eyes of a man who had spent his whole life on the sea.

"Might 'pear normal enough, Cap'n, but I have my doubts. Sumpin' in my innards says it's not what it seems to be. Can't put my finger on it, though."

"Look," he observed, pointing his finger again. "See how heavy she's sittin' in the water? And if she's cargo, why is she anchored so far out?"

"Could be she's just arrived and hasn't moved in to unload," returned Captain Jarden thoughtfully.

"Might be," Caleb rejoined, "but I have my 'spicions after all that talk we heard in England 'bout the French and Indians joinin' forces with the Continentals."

"Don't rule out pirates either. Well, whoever it is, Caleb, they saw us hoist our colors."

Both men closely observed the transport sitting quietly at anchor as they sailed by. Beyond it, they could see the dim outline of another ship. From the shape, it appeared to be a frigate. Neither spoke until they were well beyond the vessels. A man of great strength, Captain Jarden covered his concern with a clipped order.

"Post a round-the-clock watch with armed men, and have the cannons ready if needed. We may have a boarding party."

With a great heave of his chest, he turned away to go to his quarters. Rosa followed, waiting until the door was closed before she spoke.

"What is it, Father? What does all this mean?"

"I'm not sure, Rosa," he replied, choosing his words carefully. "It may be only a cargo ship. If so, we have nothing to

fear. But we're living in a time of great change for our homeland, and anything can happen. Castine may be attacked. The
powers that be in Boston are not too happy with the British occupation here. They've been raiding the supply ships up and
down the coasts. I want you to stay close to the house for a
few days until we see what's afoot."

Rosa nodded her head with lowered glance. She had
hoped to ride her beloved Nightstar over toward the Giles'
farm in hopes of seeing John. The thought of him brought a
blush to stain her cheeks. She had been gone so long—would
he even remember her? She looked up quickly to see if her father had noted her disappointment, but he was busy getting
some of his things together to take ashore.

That accomplished, he stood staring at the bed where her
mother had spent her final hours. Rosa felt her heart sicken as
she watched the transformation of his features. Lost for a moment in his grief, he turned away with a great shuddering sigh.

"Come, Rosa—get together what you wish to take
ashore," he said with constricting voice. "We need to do what
has to be done."

Rosa sought the sanctuary of the small room just off the
captain's quarters that had afforded many pleasurable hours
while accompanying her father and mother on their many voy-
ages. Most of her possessions had been packed earlier, so there
was little to do other than pick up the small brocade valise
containing several new books she had brought back with her.
Caleb would see to bringing the rest later. With a quick glance
around the neat room, she carefully closed the door and hurried to join her father. An anemic sun was struggling to penetrate the thick layers of fog.

Rosa stared with fascination at the strange vessel now
barely visible. A brief appearance of the sun glinted from
something there. Although she could see no one, still she believed they were the subject of curious eyes.

"Father, someone on that ship is watching us through
their glass," she whispered.

"I know, Rosa—I saw it too," he answered quietly through tightened lips. "It's bearing the name *Flying Fish.* Have you ever heard of her, Caleb?"

"Can't say I have, Cap'n. Don't you be worryin' your purty head about such things, lass," Caleb teased, trying to appear cheerful. "It's probably some sailor tryin' to catch a look at the likes of you." But Rosa was not so easily fooled. The grim expression on his face belied the words he spoke.

Without comment, she watched as her father climbed down into the small boat that would take them ashore. Then accepting Caleb's assistance, she was lowered into her father's waiting arms.

"Cap'n, I'll take care of things here and be in with the . . . uh, the rest of your belongin's later." He cleared his throat noisily, a shadow passing over his countenance.

Rosa's glance found her father's as both knew that Caleb alluded to the job of bringing her mother's body home. Grimly, Captain Jarden gave the order to push off.

Caleb gazed after them while the gap between the boats widened. He waved in response to Rosa's farewell. He had been with Captain Jarden for many years, and they were family. Sharing their grief seemed very natural to him, for he had loved and respected the captain's wife. It was he who had seen to her comfort when she shared a voyage with her husband. Cupping his hands around his mouth, he shouted to the young seaman rowing them ashore.

"You return 'board ship immediately, Tobias, or I'll have yer head!"

When there was no response, he turned away to begin the task of securing the ship and tending to the gruesome task of getting the body of Mrs. Jarden ashore.

During the brief ride to shore, Rosa found her thoughts returning again and again to the strange ship resting at anchor outside the harbor. A strange premonition that this vessel boded no good invaded her consciousness. Turning her face landward, she fought off the dark mood that threatened to ruin her homecoming.

Would John Giles have seen their ship sail into the harbor from high on the bluff where his father's farm was? Was she expecting too much that he might be there to greet her? Her eyes searched for his familiar face among the men standing under the big hemlock tree near the tavern. Her heart was sinking with disappointment when she caught sight of his tall figure, striding down the hill, hat in hand. His face gleamed in the morning light as he stopped near a tree. British soldiers were everywhere, some watching their approach with interest.

Glancing quickly to see her father's attention was diverted, she ventured to wave her handkerchief at him. His quick response set her heart pounding, bringing heat to her face. Suddenly shy, she pulled the hood of her cloak over her face.

As the small boat neared shore, she saw John leave his covert and walk toward them, taking a position a short distance away. It took every nerve in her body to remain quiet while Tobias secured the dinghy.

Her father stepped ashore and turned to help her, taking note of her flushed countenance. A smile faded from the innocent face of Tobias as he received an undeserved, stern, accusing scowl from his superior. Confused and uncertain, he beat a hasty departure.

"Come, Rosa—I'll see you to the house," Captain Jarden said abruptly, taking her arm to lead her through the gaping crowd. One soldier, a handsome lieutenant, was bold in his appraisal, angering Captain Jarden, who shouldered his way past him.

Rosa could only glance in John's direction as she was hurried along by her father's firm grasp. His eyes held hers briefly, setting off a tumult in her breast, and she dropped her head to hide her feeling, lest she betray herself.

Their home, halfway up the hill on the main road leading from the harbor, was but a short walk. Rosa always thrilled at the sight of the stately two-story building with its Corinthian columns supporting a covered porch above a wide veranda below. Numerous large windows gave each room a bright, airy atmosphere and a commanding view of the bay. It was here Captain Jarden had brought his young English bride to begin their lives together, and here Rosa was born.

Again this thought of her mother brought the tears that always seemed so close to the surface these days. A quick glance at her father's grim face let her know this homecoming was very painful for him as well.

Entering the gate, Captain Jarden avoided the front entrance, choosing instead to walk the curved path leading to the kitchen adjoining the main house. Calinta was waiting at the door for them, her black face wreathed in a white-toothed welcome. Her smile faded in alarm when she detected that Mrs. Jarden was not present with them.

"Wh' yo' missus, Cap'n Jarden?—how come she not wi' yo'?" she asked, her eyes passing from Rosa's tear-stained cheeks to the captain's grief-stricken face.

"She's gone, Cally; she became ill about three days out on our return from England," he choked out.

The stunned African woman held her arms wide for Rosa, who fled there for comfort, while Captain Jarden disappeared into the other part of the house.

Later, in her room downstairs, Rosa could hear him pacing the floor of the bedroom overhead that he had shared with her mother. The footsteps would pause every now and then before the window facing the harbor. How much time had passed before she heard him descend the stairs she did not know. The warm bath and hot tea Calinta had fixed for her were relaxing, and the last thing she remembered was the sound of voices at the rear of the house. It was only when Calinta was shaking her awake she realized she had fallen asleep.

"Missy Rosa—Cap'n say come! I hep yo'," she said gently, laying out clothes.

Knowing that her father was an impatient man, Rosa

quickly dressed and presented herself in the sitting room, where Captain Jarden stood looking out over the bay.

"You will need your shawl, Rosa," he said, turning as she entered. A frown creased his forehead as he gave her an appraising look. "How like your mother you are!"

Not knowing how to respond, Rosa stood still before him. She knew without asking that the time had come for her mother's burial.

"Here's Calinta with your cape. We must go."

The walk to the small cemetery was taken in silence as they seemed locked in their own thoughts. Caleb was already there with several crewmen standing by a cart bearing a long wooden box. Beyond them at a respectable distance stood several of the town's people. After it dawned on her that the box bore the body of her mother, Rosa could not bring herself to look at it again.

She became aware of a terrible feeling in the pit of her stomach, leaving her shaking and cold. What was she going to do? Panic assailed her, and she fought off the desire to run back to her room and hide her face under the covers as she used to do when she was afraid of a storm. At the sight of the gaping hole in the ground, her steps faltered. Captain Jarden tightened his hold reassuringly on her arm.

"You'll be all right, Rosa. This will take only a few moments."

With a nod at Caleb, he removed his hat. The men lifted the box from the cart and lowered it carefully with ropes into the grave. Captain Jarden waited until the men had returned to their places, then scooped up a handful of soil.

"Almighty God, we return this soul lovingly into your care. We . . . we will miss her." His voice broke. "Uh . . . give us the strength to go on without her. Amen."

The dirt released from her father's hand resounded loudly on the lid of the coffin, breaking the solemn silence. Somewhere behind Rosa, she heard a quiet sob. Replacing his hat, Captain Jarden led Rosa away. They had gone but a short distance when he instructed Rosa to wait there, while he returned to talk with Caleb and his men.

Though she scarcely knew any of them, Rosa acknowledged the condolences of those who had come to pay their last respects to her mother. When they had gone, she stood looking out across the water with unseeing eyes. Suddenly aware there was another presence near, she looked around to see John Giles beside her.

"I heard about your ma—I'm sorry," he offered timidly. "It must be hard to lose your mother. I'd miss mine somethin' terrible."

Rosa nodded her head, glancing back at her father, still talking earnestly with Caleb. The latter seemed upset, gesturing with both hands.

"I've missed you, Rosa. I've been watchin' every day for your father's ship. I'm glad you're home."

Rosa felt her heart leap in her breast. A shyness overtook her, and color mounted to her cheeks. Not knowing how to respond, she stared at the brown leaves at her feet. It wasn't proper to let a young man know how much you cared. She could feel his puzzled gaze on her face.

When no response was apparent, he cleared his throat and stammered, "Like I said, I'm sorry about your ma." He stood there a moment, uncertain of what to do, then turned to go.

Startled at his singular action, Rosa found her voice. "John, wait! I—I was going to ride out your way to see you—you all, soon."

"No, Rosa, you mustn't!" he warned. "Things have changed."

"You mean, you—you don't like me anymore?" she asked, taken aback by his answer.

"No. It isn't that," he denied heatedly, gray eyes becoming serious. "Things have changed between our two countries. You've been away so long you probably haven't heard. The colonies are at war with the British. There's fightin' going on south of us, and Pa says we're takin' a stand with the Continentals and will fight for freedom. He doesn't want me 'sociatin' with no Tory."

"John, you know I'm no Tory!" Rosa stomped her foot in exasperation. "You know Castine is my home, and I love it."

"I know that, Rosa, but Pa doesn't. He says you're British and will stand by the crown."

"Little he knows," she retorted.

"Your pa's comin'. Meet me at the rocks in that little thicket of spruce on the old path to the bluff. Come when the sun is high. I'll wait every day. Pa's usually nappin' then."

Rosa could hear her father's footsteps crunching in the stony ground behind her. John calmly greeted him and bowed to Rosa.

"My sympathy is with yuh, Captain Jarden. Good day, Miss Jarden."

Rosa turned away so that her father could not directly see her face. Captain Jarden frowned after the round-limbed, youthful figure striding away.

"Now, what was that all about, Rosa?"

"He was just offering his condolences, Father."

"Isn't that the son of Tom Giles? . . . Wonder how he knew?" he mused. "No matter. I keep forgetting how news travels in Castine."

"I think so, Father," Rosa answered, striving to keep her tone light. She took hold of his arm as they walked back down the hill.

"Good man, Tom Giles. Stubborn but honest. Haven't seen him much of late. I tried to hire him, but he never took to the sea. Had his heart set on farming."

"Father, there's talk of a revolution. I heard someone say that the colonies to the south are wanting freedom from British rule. There's talk that the fighting has already started. If we're at war, what will it mean?"

The captain stopped midstride. "I was hoping this news wouldn't reach your ears, Rosa."

"What will it mean?" she repeated, studying his face.

"Mean?" He took her small hands in his strong grasp as he thoughtfully considered her question. Glancing over his shoulder to see if they were alone, he continued, "It means I will have to take sail immediately to avoid arrest. I have been delivering supplies to Boston, and the British will not take kindly to it. There's a chance they don't know about it yet."

"I was hoping not to have to go back to sea for a while," Rosa responded hopefully.

"You'll not need to. Caleb is insisting we take you with us, but pirates and raiding British ships are making it increasingly more dangerous on the high seas. You'll be safer here with Calinta and Shonto. The British will not harm you. Just stay in the house and don't ride the trails. Caleb says there's talk of the British encouraging Indian raids against those thought to sympathize with the dissidents.

"Keep your wits about you, Daughter, and be strong. I'll not be able to come back until the war is over. I'll try to get word to you, somehow. Come—we must hurry."

There was no further conversation between them as they walked on. The sun had disappeared behind a cloud, and the wind had increased, biting at her cheeks. Rosa drew her cape tighter around her to keep out a chill that was not altogether due to the weather. The warmth of the kitchen when they stepped through the door was welcome. Calinta had hot tea and cakes ready. Her father did not sit, but remained standing to sip his tea, staring out the window toward the sea. He waved aside the cakes Calinta offered him. Setting his cup down, he excused himself and went to his room. Rosa could hear the floor creak as he moved about. His steps seemed hurried.

"Cap'n goin' go back t' sea," Calinta lamented, shaking her head. "Good yo' stay here."

"I'm staying," Rosa replied.

"Fo' once yo' pa show some sense. Wimmin got no call t' go t' sea. Yo' mama stay home, be 'live," Calinta soliloquized, nodding her head to emphasize her feelings as she moved around lighting the lamps.

Thickening clouds were causing the evening to set in early, and Rosa knew her father would soon leave under the cover of darkness. No one would be expecting him to sail so soon, and with no moon or stars he could escape undetected.

Upstairs, Captain Jarden looked around the room he had shared with his wife. Everything in it reflected the love and care that had been theirs. Most had been gifts he had brought back from far countries across the sea. The mahogany chair by the window spoke loudly of her presence. He lit the lamp on the table beside it and sat down. Remembering the many times he had relaxed on the bed watching the lamplight play upon her hair caused him to drop his head into his hands. A great shuddering sob vented the sorrow and longing within.

Finally, drained and weary, he brushed the hair away from his face and reached for his hat. It was growing dark; the time to leave was near. Leaving Rosa would be difficult, but it was for the best. With a deep sigh, he picked up his sea bag, blew out the lamp, then descended the stairs.

Rosa was waiting for him in the kitchen. She rose to her feet expectantly as he entered the room. The wide-eyed Calinta was hovering nearby, hands entangled in her apron.

"Father, I will miss you so."

"And I you, Daughter. But this time it is better you stay here. There will be less danger." He kissed her on the cheek and touched her hair. "How like your mother you are!" he said again, his voice husky. "We shall both miss her."

"Take good care of her, Calinta," he implored, looking over Rosa's head. "She's all I have now. Tell Shonto to get plenty of firewood in. Caleb brought supplies from the ship."

He had changed his captain's coat and hat in favor of a warm short jacket such as was worn by most seamen. Pulling a knit hat low over his forehead, he glanced around the room as if burning it in his memory.

"Turn down the lamps, Cally," he instructed, waiting for

her to comply. Then, opening the door, he stepped into the chill of the night. Rosa followed him out.

"Good-bye, Father," she whispered. "Come back to me."

He squeezed her hand and was gone; his tall figure with its broad shoulders faded quickly into the shadows. In spite of the cold, and unable to help herself, Rosa followed as far as the gate. Down the street, British soldiers were standing guard at their headquarters at Mullet Block. She saw her father cross the street to join a group of sailors who appeared to have had more than enough to drink, just as a detail of British soldiers came out and started up the hill.

Suddenly, the feeling she would never see her father again swept over her, and she started to call after him, but the approaching redcoats caused her to hold her tongue. She watched until he vanished in the darkness. Her mind went to the ships she had observed earlier that brought the same strong premonition of something terrible and frightening.

"Chile, yo' get yo'sef back in dis house fo' yo' catch a chill," Calinta called from the lighted doorway.

Trembling uncontrollably, Rosa turned and fled into the arms of the waiting woman.

"Chile, wh' fo' yo' shakin'!"

"Oh, Cally, he's not coming back."

"Sssh!" Calinta said, drawing the distraught girl inside.

Leading Rosa to a chair by the fire, she returned to lock and bar the door. "Dark has ears. Now, yo' say to Cally wassa matta."

Rosa was relating the story of the strange ship and her feelings, purposely leaving out the part involving John Giles, when a noise at the service door leading into the stables caused her to falter. She gave a fearful glance up at Calinta, who picked up a piece of wood to hold it high above her head. As the door inched open, the woman stood ready to strike.

A black face appeared in the light, bringing a loud burst of relief from Calinta. It was Shonto, Calinta's only surviving relative. Stolen from their native land, they had been forced into the hold of a slave ship. When it had wrecked on a reef during a storm, most had been drowned, still in their chains.

Miraculously, Calinta and Shonto had been thrown free when the ship broke apart. They were barely alive, clinging to pieces of wreckage, when Captain Jarden rescued them. They had been a part of the Jarden household ever since.

"Wh' fo' yo' come sneakin' in heah, Shonto?" Calinta scolded, throwing the stick of wood on the pile. "Yo' scare Miss Rosa t' def!"

"Bad things goin' on out theah," the young man croaked, his eyes rolling with excitement.

"What yo' sayin' 'bout?" Calinta demanded, drawing him into the light.

Shonto answered, making a circular motion: "Redcoats come to arrest Cap'n. Stay round house. Tell Shonto no one leave. They take horses."

"Nightstar!" Rosa cried, jumping to her feet in alarm. "Did they take Nightstar?" When the boy nodded his answer, Rosa was stunned. Her father had given Nightstar to her on her 14th birthday.

Never would she forget that day. Captain Jarden had instructed her to remain with her mother on the terrace. While she waited with eyes closed, anticipation turned into excitement as she heard the unmistakable sounds of a horse coming toward her. She could scarcely wait until she was told to open her eyes. Pressing the reins into her hand, her parents wished her a happy birthday. She looked up to see a sleek black mare with a white star emblazoned on her forehead standing there. On her back was a beautiful black saddle of the finest hand-tooled leather.

"Oh, you beautiful thing!" she cried. "Father, what is her name?"

"Your mother thought you would want to name her."

The horse moved closer, nuzzling Rosa's hand, allowing her to stroke its velvety nose and touch the star.

"It shall be Star. No! I'll call her Nightstar."

Until this present time, no one had ever ridden Nightstar but her. Most certainly they would not do so now. They shall not get away with this, she vowed, silently, anger surging through her. The nerve of them!

"Chile, wh' yo' thinkin'?" Calinta queried, noting the change that had come over Rosa.

"Cally, tomorrow I'm going to get Nightstar back," was Rosa's resolute response.

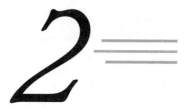

THE SUN WAS ALREADY HIGH when Rosa opened her eyes the next morning. A fire, started in the hearth to drive away the chill, was a welcome sight. Rolling on her back, she stared up at the ceiling. How many times she had remained in such a state listening to the murmur of voices overhead, her mother's happy laughter and the sound of her light step!

How quickly it had all ended! So suddenly she was without a mother, and now she did not know if she would ever see her father again. Somehow she must find the courage to go on. After all, she had Cally and Shonto, a comfortable home, and there was John.

Calinta came in to poke up the fire. Throwing on another piece of wood, she turned, hands on hips, to look at Rosa. "Missy Rosa, yo' gon' t' sleep mos' day? Sun half high."

Rosa smiled, as she always did, at Calinta's way of telling time. "Cally, lay out one of my best dresses—I'll be paying a visit to Nightstar's captors, and I want to look my best," Rosa instructed, slipping from under the covers.

"Missy, dem redcoats no let you outta house."

"Oh, they will, Cally," Rosa assured her with great emphasis. "You can stake your life on it. In fact, they'll not only let me out but escort me to their headquarters."

Reluctantly, Calinta helped her dress; then, grumbling under her breath, she headed for the kitchen. Rosa purposed in her mind just what she must say. Surveying herself in the mirror, she was pleased with the golden-haired image in a blue dress staring back at her. Though she had inherited her father's strong will and fire, her face bore the characteristics of her mother's delicate beauty. Serious brown eyes belied the inner turmoil she felt.

Satisfied with her appearance, she turned away to pick up her shawl but stopped. It would not do to wear the dark heavy shawl. She needed something more dressy—no, something to make her appear older. But what? Her mind went to the beautiful coat in her mother's closet. Dare she?

It took only a moment to quietly mount the stairs. She paused at the doorway, hesitant to invade the privacy of her father's domain, knowing full well that if he were here she would receive a stern reprimand. But the thought of poor Nightstar drove her on.

The knob turned easily in her hand, and she pushed the door open. Still lingering in the room was the odor of her father's pipe. Looking around, she noted the bed had been undisturbed. A book her mother had been reading remained open on the table beside her favorite chair. It was a small Bible. The well-worn pages spoke of her mother's simple but profound faith in a providential God. Rosa picked it up and held it to her breast. Many of the stories in this Book Elizabeth Jarden had read to Rosa as a young child.

Calinta's call to breakfast jarred her back to the present. Tucking the Bible under her arm, she searched in vain through her mother's wardrobe. Thinking back to when she had last seen her mother wear the coat, Rosa remembered it was in England. She was about to decide it had been left aboard ship when her eyes fell on a seabag on the floor by the door. It was her mother's. Caleb had brought their things ashore while she was resting yesterday.

Rosa opened it with trembling fingers. The coat was there along with other items of clothing. Before lifting it out, her hands caressed the white fox-fur collar adorning the white brocade bodice.

"Missy Rosa, yo' up deah wh' yo' no 'spose t' be?" Calinta called up the stairs. "Yo' eatin' gettin' hard!"

"I'm coming right down, Cally," Rosa answered, heading that way. She paused at the door of her room to drop off the borrowed articles before hurrying on to the kitchen, where she was met with a disapproving glance from Calinta.

"When Cap'n say take care of yo', he say, biiiig job!" she grumbled, rolling her eyes heavenward and gesturing her surrender to the inevitable.

"Oh, Cally, don't go on so!" Rosa chided with a grin. "I'm just borrowing mother's coat for a little while. Someone has to do something about getting our horses back, and I'm the only one who can." She took a sip of her tea before going on. "Besides, Father said the British wouldn't harm me. I think he would expect me to rescue Nightstar and the others."

No reply was forthcoming from Calinta, who busied herself with her chores. Rosa ate her food slowly and thoughtfully, watching the dark-skinned woman move about. She and Shonto had been with them as long as she could remember, yet she knew little about the early years Calinta and Shonto had spent in their native land.

"Cally, do you ever wish to be back with your own people—to go back to your home?"

Calinta turned, water dripping from her fingers, to give Rosa a long, searching look. "Why Missy Rosa ask?"

"I just wondered," Rosa replied with candor. "You've never talked of your homeland."

Calinta wrapped her wet hands in the long apron tied around her waist and stared wistfully out the window. A red-coated soldier walked past, and they both watched until he was out of sight.

"When Cap'n brought us heah, I sick heah," Calinta said, putting her hand over her heart. "Cap'n and Miss Liz'beth good t' Calinta an' Shonto. He say he take back, someday. Me no go back. Shonto no go back. Bad man come take ag'in. Our home here. Yo' our people."

Calinta went back to her work, leaving Rosa touched deeply by her words. There was no doubt in her mind that her father and mother had been patient and kind in teaching them their ways. Now that her mother was gone and her father would be at sea, it was up to Rosa to care for them.

"Cally, would you like to learn to read?" Rosa asked, taking the last sip of her tea.

"Re . . . ad?" Calinta paused to gaze at Rosa in wonder. "Wha' Missy say?"

"Wait! I'll show you," Rosa exclaimed, leaving the table to get the Bible from her room. Returning quickly, she held it out for Calinta to see. "Calinta, would you like to know what this Book says?"

Calinta looked from Rosa to the Book in her hand. Then a smile broke across her face. "Yo' say to Calinta wha' Book say?"

"Cally, I'll teach you and Shonto to say what the Book says. We will start tonight. It will give us something to do. Would you like that?"

"Calinta like. Shonto like. Missy good like Cap'n." The black eyes of the woman glowed with a warm light, and tears sprang to the surface and trickled down her dark, shiny cheeks.

"Then it's settled. I must go now. Have Shonto bring the person in charge of these soldiers to me. I'll wait in the parlor."

Rosa went to her room and donned her mother's coat, then, taking her best bonnet, she tucked her hair in place, leaving a few strands to accent her face. Satisfied that she presented a striking appearance, she retired to the settee in the parlor to wait. It was only a matter of moments before a tap sounded at the front door. Calinta went to answer, swinging the door wide.

"I was told a Miss Rosa wished to see me?" Rosa heard a masculine voice say with clipped British accent.

"Show him in, Cally," Rosa spoke up with measured tone.

Calinta stepped back, allowing him to enter. It was plain by her demeanor she was not pleased with the prospect of having the enemy in her home.

Rosa's heart felt as if it was in her throat. She swallowed hard, hoping her nervousness would not show. Her eyes widened as his tall frame filled the doorway. Then he was there standing before her. As he bowed slightly, his dark eyes boldly raked over her, coming to rest again on her face, causing the color to heighten in her cheeks.

"You are staring, sir," Rosa admonished haughtily, standing to her feet.

"I beg your pardon, Miss—it's just that I haven't seen anyone so beautiful for a long time," he responded smoothly, removing his hat to expose a shock of black hair. His narrowed glance had a strange glint as a sardonic smile spread across his handsome face. "What is it you wish to see me about?"

Though sheltered and protected by her father and Caleb in the presence of other men, Rosa instinctively knew this man was accustomed to women succumbing to his good looks and charm, and it angered her, causing a slight edge in her voice.

"What has become of our horses?"

"They have been confiscated for use in the British army."

"Where are they? I want them brought back immediately."

"I'm afraid I cannot do that," he answered stiffly.

"Then who can?" she demanded impatiently.

"You will have to talk to the one who gave the order. I'm sure that will do you no good, though. We need those horses."

"We shall see. Will you take me to him, uh . . . ."

"Lieutenant Pennington at your service, Miss. If you wish, I can escort you to headquarters. When did you wish to go?"

"I am ready now, sir."

"My name is Howland; my friends call me Howie," he informed her, holding out his elbow for her to take.

"'Sir' will do quite nicely," she rejoined, ignoring his arm as she swept past him into the cold, crisp air.

The short walk down the hill to Mullet House, where the

officers were quartered, was exhilarating, clearing her head. They entered the building amid admiring stares from the men loitering on the steps.

Rosa was told to wait in the outer office while the lieutenant disappeared down the hallway, his boots making a hollow sound on the bare wooden floor. A door opened and closed. Then all was silent, save for the scratching of a pen used by a soldier seated at a table.

Aware of the covert glances he kept casting in her direction, Rosa looked around the room. Other than the makeshift desk, there were few furnishings. Several chairs lined the wall, and a small stove with a coffeepot on top of it gave off a welcome warmth. She turned expectantly at the sound of a door opening. Lieutenant Pennington approached to tell her Captain Mowatt would see her now. Following him, Rosa was certain her request had already been discussed. Armed with the knowledge Nightstar's fate depended on the outcome of this meeting, she resolved to keep her wits, though her legs quaked beneath her. Lieutenant Pennington ushered her into the presence of a sandy-haired man, graying at the temples, with clear, piercing blue eyes. Rosa guessed him to be in his 50s, about the same age as her father.

"That will be all, Lieutenant," he said briskly, dismissing his subordinate. Rising to his feet, he came around the desk, fingers unconsciously checking the buttons of his immaculate red jacket as he bowed slightly.

"Good day, Miss Jarden. My name is Captain Mowatt; I am at your service. Please be seated." He indicated one of two chairs in front of the desk, waiting until she was comfortable before continuing. "I understand you wish to see me about some horses conscripted for use in the British army."

Rosa studied his face as he was speaking. It was a nice face, but stern, every inch that of a dedicated soldier. She stiffened at his reference to taking the horses.

"*Stolen* is the word, Captain Mowatt," she said with spirit. "Your men broke into our barn and took our horses. One of them was Nightstar, the mare my father gave me for my birthday. No one has ever ridden her except me. I want her back." Though her voice was steady, her hands were trembling. She kept them hidden in the folds of her skirt.

"Is your father ill? Why did he send you to take care of this matter?" he asked pointedly.

"My father is not here. After we buried my mother, he could not stand to be in the house." She lowered her eyes to stare at the toe of her dainty highbuttoned shoe. "He sailed out with his men last evening," she went on in a voice that was barely audible.

The captain stared at her in disbelief, then abruptly stepped to look out the window toward the harbor. Jarden's ship was gone. Why had such a thing escaped his attention? He had ordered the house surrounded. How could he have gotten away? He should have arrested the man as he returned from the grave, but out of respect for his dead wife and for his daughter, who accompanied him, he had delayed such an order, choosing instead to post a watch and remove the horses to assure that he could not slip away in the dark to make his way over land to a friendly port.

He returned to his chair and lowered his bulky weight into the seat. It was not easy to admit you had been outfoxed in the presence of this slip of a woman. He stared at Rosa, who sat in wide-eyed innocence before him, returning his gaze calmly, waiting for him to speak again. He sat drumming his fingers.

"Are you aware your father is providing supplies to the insurgents?" he asked finally, in a cold harsh voice.

"Sir, my father sails to many ports. I do not question his actions."

"But you sail with him, do you not?"

"Yes, Captain. My mother and I accompanied him to England on his last trip to visit her relatives. We were on our way home from there when she died."

"You are not afraid of me, are you?"

"No, Captain Mowatt. My father told me I had nothing to fear from you—that you would not harm me."

"He did, did he?" The captain gave a short laugh, shaking his shaggy head. Captain Jarden was certainly an interesting character, and this daughter of his was smart, as well as beautiful. His sternness softened a little as he thought about his own daughter back in England.

"Captain Mowatt, what about Nightstar?" Rosa persisted, with pleading, unwavering eyes. "If you do not wish to return Charger, please let me have my beloved Nightstar back."

He did not answer, but got up and left the room. When he returned he announced, "Lieutenant Pennington will escort you home."

"But what about Nightstar?" she implored earnestly, standing quickly to her feet.

His silence was a dismissal. It was as if she were no longer there. He had turned his attention back to his work. Lieutenant Pennington appeared at the door.

"See to it," Captain Mowatt instructed gruffly, not looking up from the paper he held in his hand.

Rosa looked from one to the other, realizing further conversation was useless. Lieutenant Pennington's hand pressing on her arm let her know it was time to go. Disappointment overwhelmed her as she allowed herself to be led out.

On the short walk back to the house, several attempts by the lieutenant to make conversation were met with stony silence. Troubled and near tears, Rosa was in no mood to be amiable.

Poor Nightstar. She had failed to gain the mare's release. A feeling of helplessness assailed her. What had happened to the safe, orderly world she knew such a short time ago? Was this all part of the terrible premonition she had felt earlier? Suddenly she felt very alone. Why did her mother and father leave her here by herself? Anger came to her rescue as she fought back tears threatening to erupt.

Circumstances had dealt her a terrible blow, but she

would survive. She must! Calinta and Shonto needed her. By the time they reached the gate, Rosa had pulled herself together enough to manage a weak smile for her surprised escort.

"Thank you, Lieutenant—I apologize for my behavior," she said, extending her hand. "My horse Nightstar means a great deal to me. It's not easy to give her up. I hope they will treat her kindly. She has never known a whip or spur."

Rosa left him then, aware his puzzled gaze followed her. Choosing not to enter the front, she went around to the side entrance, where she was confronted by a soldier stationed there.

"Lieutenant Pennington," she called back, trying to control the anger in her voice, "please get these men off my property. There is no need for them to be here. We are no threat to you."

"Step aside, Corporal," was the curt order.

Rosa saw Calinta's troubled face at the window, and then the door opened for her to enter. Once inside, she gave a long, shuddering sigh before answering the unspoken question in Calinta's face.

"I'm . . . I'm all right, Cally. They treated me well. But I didn't get poor Nightstar back." Rosa's voice broke at this point.

"Missy, yo' feel bad. Yo' cry. Be awright. Yo' lotsa cry 'bout," Calinta crooned, taking the weeping girl into her arms.

"Cally, what has happened to us?" Rosa sobbed. "Mother and Father are both gone, and now Nightstar. Our lives will never be the same again. Has God forsaken me?"

"Missy, Shonto an' Calinta wi' be safe. Yo' jes' missin' yo' folk 'n hoss." Calinta pushed Rosa away so that she could look her in the face. A warm glow entered her dark, velvety eyes as she wiped Rosa's tears away with the corner of her apron.

"Missy Rosa, yo' has Cap'n's blood. Calinta, Shonto trust yo'. We fam'ly. Yo' good, 'n' yo' do good. Yo' see."

"Thank you, Cally—you encourage me. Losing Nightstar is hard for me to accept, along with all the other, but I'll make it. We'll come through this together. Tell Shonto we will begin your lessons after tea. Right now, I need to change my dress and put mother's coat away."

"Redcoats with guns gone," Shonto informed them when he joined them later to begin the lesson.

"Good!" Rosa exclaimed, surprised that she hadn't noticed their departure. "At least my visit accomplished something!"

"I told them Father was gone—you should have seen Captain Mowatt's face when he heard the news," she continued with a giggle. "He hadn't even missed the ship. Mercy—I don't know how they expect to win a war."

The afternoon hours sped by as Rosa patiently instructed Calinta and Shonto in the alphabet. Holding the quill pens was strange and difficult for them at first, but soon they mastered the art of making some legible marks on the paper. It would be slow, she thought, watching them labor over their letters, but it was evident she would have plenty of time.

"Would you like for me to read you a story?" she asked finally.

Both sat in rapt attention as she read them a story she had chosen from her mother's Bible. It was the story of Joseph, who was sold into slavery by his brothers.

"Wh' fo' dey do 'at, Missy Rosa?" Shonto asked.

"For the same reason those men took you from your homeland and brought you here to be sold as slaves, Shonto— they were bad in here," Rosa answered, pointing to her heart. "But God is good, and He helped Joseph."

"Cap'n good like yo' God," Calinta stated simply, rising to her feet. "Cap'n hep Calinta, hep Shonto."

"Cally, Father is good because our God, yours and mine, lives in his heart."

Calinta gave Rosa a strange look and turned away. "Missy Rosa say words Calinta don' know." She gave Shonto a command in their native tongue and walked out.

After they had gone, Rosa pondered Calinta's parting remark as she gathered up the lesson materials and placed them on a shelf. Why had Cally responded like that? Like most seafaring people, her father had referred many times to God's providence in Cally's presence. The name would not be unfamiliar to her. Oh, well—she would pursue the matter another time. Right now she was too weary.

Stretching out on the bed to rest, her thoughts turned to John. Without Nightstar, there was no way she could meet him. Had he waited for her today? Her heart beat faster at the remembrance of his solemn promise to wait for her each day in hopes she would come.

Dreamily, she imagined what such a meeting would be like and found herself blushing. They had never been alone before. On her visits to the farm there had always been family around. She had often taken books to read to his sisters. Only once he had dared to hold her hand as he walked her to the gate. A sweetness filled her as she recalled his touch.

"Missy Rosa, Missy Rosa, yo' come," called Calinta as she burst into the room where Rosa was.

"What is it, Cally?" Rosa cried in alarm, jumping to her feet.

Calinta's eyes were round with excitement, her arms flailing the air.

"Yo' come! Shonto say come!"

As Rosa hesitated, Calinta took her by the hand, pulling her along to the kitchen and on through the storage room to the barn. Shonto stood by the door of Nightstar's stable with shining eyes.

"Look, Missy Rosa! Nightstar!" he urged, pointing into the stall.

Joy and wonder filled her heart as she ran to the door. There stood her beloved mare, saddle and all.

"Nightstar! You're back!" Rosa cried as the mare whinnied a welcome. She rushed to circle the horse's neck with her arms. "Oh, my precious Nightstar—I thought I had lost you! Did they hurt you? Shonto, remove the saddle and check her flanks."

Rosa ran her fingers along Nightstar's coat to find a long welt. "Oh, Shonto, they've whipped her! Look! There's dried blood! I'll get some water and cleanse her wounds. You get the salve."

Returning with warm water and clean cloths, Rosa found Shonto had already removed the saddle, revealing long, deep scratches where someone had raked the mare with spurs. Tears coursed down Rosa's cheeks as she washed away the dried blood. She stayed until the job was completed and Nightstar was contentedly munching oats.

ROSA OPENED HER EYES to find the sun shining brightly through her bedroom window. For the past several days since Nightstar's return a cold rain had been falling. Not that it mattered; the mare had been in no condition to ride anyway. But now she welcomed the change. Perhaps today she could take her out.

The thought spurred her to action. Throwing back the covers, she sought the warmth of the fire Calinta had thoughtfully laid. The chill of the room set her teeth to chattering as she was forced to leave the blaze to find something to wear. Selecting a wool riding skirt, boots, and a heavy sweater, she quickly dressed, cold fingers fumbling with the buttons. The water in the basin on the wash stand was so icy she had about decided against washing her face when Calinta entered with a steaming kettle. She flashed a white-toothed smile at the shivering girl huddled before the fire.

"Missy up wi' sun—good sign," she acknowledged, nodding her head.

"I think I'll take Nightstar out for a ride later today." Rosa spoke casually, without looking up.

The sound of hot water pouring into the basin stopped. The crackling of the fire sounded loud in the dead silence that followed as Calinta paused to give Rosa a long look.

"Missy no go," she said firmly. "Shonto go."

"Now don't go making a fuss, Cally," Rosa coaxed. "I promise I'll not go far or stay long. I haven't been able to ride Nightstar since my return, and I refuse to become a prisoner in this house."

"Yo' jes gonna ketch yo' def," Calinta grumbled, softening.

"I'll dress warm enough, Cally," Rosa laughed, accepting the basin of warm water Calinta handed her. "It will be good for me to get out for a while. Please don't worry about me."

The African woman did not answer, but poked up the fire, put on another stick of wood, and left the room. Rosa knew by her demeanor that she did not approve of her going. Well, she would worry about it later. Nothing was going to affect the lighthearted mood she was in. Looking inward, she knew it was because she was going to see John.

She finished washing her face, then brushed her golden hair until it shone, humming happily to herself as she tied it back with a bright piece of ribbon. Studying herself in the mirror, she hoped John would find her attractive.

It took only a moment to make her bed. Then, after checking the fire, she went to join Calinta in the kitchen, where bread, wild blueberry jelly, and a steaming hot cup of tea were waiting for her.

"Thank you, Cally," said Rosa, slipping into her chair. When no acknowledgment from Calinta was forthcoming, she busied herself with eating, watching the faithful African woman shape loaves of bread and place them to rise. Shonto brought in more firewood and dropped it into the box.

"Nightstar good, Missy Rosa," he exclaimed with a broad grin.

"I'm glad to hear that, Shonto. I thought I would take her out for a ride right after we eat at noon, when the chill is off."

"She be ready," replied Shonto.

"Shonto go wi' hoss—Missy stay!" Calinta stated again, turning from the pans she was washing. The unyielding set of her mouth let both of the others know she felt strongly about Rosa's plans.

Shonto's eyes widened as he glanced from Calinta's stern face to Rosa's quiet one. Uncomfortable with the tension in the air, he started edging toward the door, feeling that it was no place for him to be at the moment. He picked up a broom and busied himself within earshot.

"Now, Cally, we've already settled the matter," Rosa beseeched good-naturedly. "Father said I could go, and I promised him I wouldn't go far."

Taking note that Calinta seemed to be relenting, she continued to plead her case. "You're worrying for nothing. What could possibly happen? Besides, Nightstar can outrun any horse in town, except Father's big Charger. The soldier who has him wouldn't have the least interest in chasing me."

"Missy no go far?" asked Calinta, giving in.

"I'll not go far."

Calinta shrugged her shoulders and returned to her work. By that, Rosa knew the issue was closed. While Calinta had her back toward her, Rosa made a sandwich from the rest of the bread, wrapped it in a napkin, and stuck it under her sweater. John would be hungry.

"I know Missy Rosa win," Shonto admitted out loud to himself, shaking his head. "Calinta no win 'gin Missy Rosa."

Rosa went to her room and replenished the fire. The long morning hours stretched endlessly before her. To help pass the time, she pulled up a chair and sat down to read one of the books she had brought back from England. But her mind kept wandering, so she soon gave it up. Laying the book aside, she decided to prepare the lesson for the afternoon.

Calinta and Shonto were doing so well with their letters she felt it was time to start them on some simple everyday words. Shonto, especially, was making great progress. During a brief walk in the garden, she had discovered letters Shonto had drawn in the dirt with a stick.

Carefully, she labored over the list, drawing pictures to illustrate each word. The crude picture of a cat made her suppress a giggle. It looked more like a cow with a long tail. Standing back to survey her work, Rosa frowned at the outcome. Clearly, she was not an artist, but it would have to do. While the ink was drying, she searched for a story to read, choosing again to find one in the Bible. Considering several options, she finally selected the story of Ruth. It had always been one of her favorites. Satisfied she had done all she could in preparation, Rosa gathered up the materials and was placing them in readiness on the shelf when Calinta called her to eat.

Rosa washed her hands and headed for the kitchen. Shonto was already there, perched on a three-legged stool by the fire.

"Shonto, is Nightstar ready?" she asked, watching Calinta ladle up a bowl of soup.

"She plenty ready."

Rosa seated herself in front of the soup. Glancing over the table, she suddenly realized the absence of meat. In fact, meat had not been a part of their diet for days. Why?

"Cally, where is the meat Father always stores up for the winter?"

"Go," Cally answered, gesturing toward the harbor.

"What do you mean, go?" insisted Rosa.

"Calinta no wanna say. No worry, Missy!"

"What is it, Cally?—tell me!" Rosa demanded, leaving the table to confront Calinta, who was taking up another bowl of hot, steaming liquid.

"Dey take—men wi' red coat take," Calinta confessed, "many days ago."

"The cow, the chickens?"

"Dey go, Missy Rosa. Soldier say dey need. Take all." Calinta gestured up and down the street.

Stunned, Rosa returned to her seat, unable to comprehend what it all meant. Why were the British robbing the people of their food? Were they cut off from their supplies? Had this happened to everyone? What about the Giles family? She must see John and find out what was going on.

Rosa was no longer hungry, but forced the hot soup down anyway. The sun was getting high. She would need to go. She went to her room for the heavy wool cape she had laid out to wear. Slipping the sandwich into one pocket and a small book of poetry she had bought for a gift to John into the other, she hurried out.

"I'll be back in a little while, Cally," she promised, walking through the kitchen on her way to the barn. The area where the chickens had been kept was silent, and Bossy's stall was empty. She was surprised she had not noticed before, yet her concern for Nightstar had been so great she had thought of little else.

Shonto had the doors open and stood stroking Nightstar to quiet her anticipation of getting out into the open. Rosa mounted with ease, giving the mare her head as she guided her toward the path leading along the high bluff overlooking the harbor. Nightstar was ready to run, and in the sheer joy of the moment Rosa forgot all her troubles. The wind bit at her cheeks as the ground raced beneath her.

"Oh, Nightstar, you wonderful creature!" she cried in exultation.

On they sped until reaching the bluff. Rosa reined her into a walk. Ahead, and to the right, was the grove of trees John had indicated. Scanning the area to see if anyone was nearby, she ducked the low-hanging branches and rode into the little glen. Her heart was beating fast at the expectation of seeing John there, but he was nowhere in sight. Perhaps he had not arrived yet. She stepped down to wait, tying the reins to a tree. Somewhere a twig snapped, and she heard a light step behind her. A cry died in her throat when she recognized John's familiar figure.

"At last, you've come!" he whispered softly, holding his fingers over his lips. Taking her by the hand, he led her into the tight space that led back into the rocks.

"It is less likely we'll be seen here," he said, dropping her hand. "Why haven't you come? I saw your father's ship was gone. I was beginnin' to think you had gone with him."

Rosa seated herself on a rock. His touch had set off such a riot of emotion in her she could scarcely stand. "We need to talk, John," she began, unsteadily. "We've had trouble."

John listened intently as she told him all that had happened since she had last seen him, leaving out what her father had told her about his activities and why he had to flee for his life. The sunlight filtering through the trees played upon her golden hair and lit up the curve of her cheek. He did not realize she had finished until he heard her ask the second time.

"What does it mean, John? Why are the British taking our stock?"

He didn't answer her question right away, staring off into space. How much could he tell her? In his heart he felt Rosa was true, even though his father declared her family's allegiance was to the crown. Had she not just returned from England, where her mother still had family ties?

He felt her questioning eyes upon him as he took a few steps away from where she sat to stand with his back to her. He did not dare betray his father and their fight for freedom. Ever since the British had taken the land away from the French, their life had been unbearable. He stood there with his hands clenched as the battle raged within him. In desperation he turned to look at her again. How beautiful she was! He had been in love with her for as long as he could remember.

"What is it, John? Why are you looking at me like that?"

He strode to kneel down before her. "Rosa, please understand what I am about to ask you. I've got to know." He paused, his grave eyes searching hers. "Are you British? Is your allegiance to the king?"

"Never!" she answered with spirit. "My mother was British until she married my father. This is our country. It is our home. We will fight for it—die for it!"

"Rumors have been spread that your father is a British spy."

"That isn't true," Rosa denied, hotly. "My father . . ." Her voice broke, and she went on in a whisper: "My father has been running supplies for the Revolutionaries. Although they had no proof, the British suspected him. As soon as he buried my mother, he had to flee, barely escaping before they came to arrest him."

Satisfied she was telling the truth, John felt he could confide in her. "I'll be back shortly. Stay here and don't make a sound no matter what happens. I'm goin' to look around."

Rosa sat listening for what seemed like a long time. Finally she could stand it no longer. Creeping to the narrow opening, she peered out. Nightstar was standing quietly, ears pointing forward. Something, or someone, was out there!

Fighting the urge to jump onto her horse and ride swiftly away, Rosa was relieved to see John coming toward her. He stopped to look around him once again before coming on toward her. How like an Indian he was! She backed away as he came through the opening in the rocks. Taking her hands, he drew her closer to him. She could feel his breath fan her cheek as he spoke urgently.

"Rosa, listen carefully to what I say. I must hurry. Father will be missin' me. General Washington is wantin' to end the British occupation of our land. He has sent some ships and men to drive the British out and take over the fort. But they haven't agreed on a plan or place to make a landin'."

"That must have been one of their ships we saw outside the harbor when we sailed in!" Rosa exclaimed. "We saw them watching us through their glass. They probably recognized the *Surgosa Rose.*"

"Could've been," John agreed, his forehead wrinkled in a frown. "They decided to wait for reinforcements before attackin' the British. Pa says the delay will only give the British time to finish the fort and make things worse.

"My pa's been secretly trainin' patriots to help when the time comes, and I am one of them," he announced proudly. "The British have been wreakin' havoc up and down the coast, attackin' our cargo ships, and with our boats blockin' the harbor, they're desperate. They must have suspected your father when he was allowed through the blockade."

"John, are we in danger?" Rosa asked, solemnly searching his face for the truth.

"I don't think so," he answered slowly, a frown forming in his serious face. "At least for now. It will depend on whether the British decide to burn us out. They aren't sure how many of us will turn against them." He got to his feet and stood looking down at her.

"Rosa, you must go. But first, there's . . . there's somethin' I want you to know," he said hesitantly, "though I have no right to say it to you."

"What is it, John?"

He dropped his head and his face turned red as she came near him, touching his sleeve.

"What are you trying to say, John?" she repeated softly, with brown eyes large and luminous in her upturned face.

"I love you," was his strangled whisper. "I can't help myself. I'll always love you, Rosa. I know that we are miles apart in life. You live in a fine house and have slaves. I'm just a farmer's son. But I wanted you to know."

Although his confession of love set her pulses stirring, she was stung by his remark about Cally and Shonto.

"John, Cally and Shonto are not slaves," she started in denial. "They . . ."

"Shhh," he warned suddenly, his head alert, listening.

When Rosa started to speak, he put a hand to her lips.

"Don't move," he said into her ear.

His steps were without sound as he moved to the opening. Outside was a British soldier sitting on his horse. His curious dark gaze was on Nightstar; then he looked all around.

"Lieutenant Pennington!" she whispered. "He must've seen me ride out in this direction and followed. It wouldn't be good for him to know you are here. I'll go out and take care of it. There's no reason for me to be afraid of him."

She gave John's hand a squeeze and slipped out, humming to herself. John saw her stop when she looked up to see the lieutenant sitting astride his horse, watching her.

"Oh, Lieutenant Pennington!—you startled me!" she cried, feigning surprise.

"I was riding by and saw your horse. I was concerned that something might have happened to you." His eyes took in the area again, coming to rest on Rosa. "Did you ride out to meet someone?" There was a ring in his voice that angered her.

"What if I did?—it would be of no concern to you," she retorted hotly. "But for your information, a person has to have a private moment once in a while. I trust you were not spying on me."

It pleased her to see the red come to his face. Untying Nightstar, she stepped gracefully into the saddle. "Now if you will allow me to pass, I would be glad to have you accompany me back to town—that is, if it was the way you were going when you happened onto my horse," was her derisive comment.

Urging Nightstar into action, she rode on ahead, then pulled up, waiting for him to catch up. Looking past him, she saw John's hand wave to her. "Nightstar, go!" she cried, leaning over the back of the mare. The horse took off, stretching out into a smooth gait. Rosa held her in check, not allowing her to run full speed and outdistance the lieutenant. It would not do for him to know how fast her mount was.

On the outskirts of town she pulled Nightstar to a walk, and the two of them rode side by side. Rosa glanced at him from under her lashes. Riding straight and tall in the saddle, Lieutenant Pennington presented a striking figure. The immaculate uniform could not hide the sheer strength of the man.

"Lieutenant, back there you told me you were concerned for my safety today. Is there a reason I should be worried?"

"Miss Jarden, I think in all fairness I should warn you there's talk of Indian activity in the area," was his meaningful reply. "It is not wise for you to be riding alone."

"Oh?—and you think you should be the one to accompany me?" she retorted. Rosa saw him stiffen as her words hit home.

"Ride with whomever you wish, my dear Miss Jarden," he said coldly. "You asked, and I warned you."

"Thank you, Lieutenant," Rosa said, smiling contritely, realizing she had been too hard on him. After all, it might pay to keep him as a friend. They had reached the road that led up the hill. Rosa reined in her horse and turned in the saddle to look at him. "I'm afraid I've been rude again, Lieutenant. Forgive me. Now, if you will excuse me, I must get on home. Cally will be worried about me."

Looking back when she was halfway up the hill, Rosa saw he was still there watching her. Instinctively, she knew this man was someone to be reckoned with. Had he been assigned to keep an eye on her? But why? Did they think her father was hiding out and that she was riding out to meet him? The lieutenant had asked if she was meeting someone, hadn't he? She dismounted and led Nightstar the rest of the way into the barn, where Shonto was waiting.

"How Nightstar go?" he asked with a grin.

"Oh, Shonto, she's the greatest!" she exclaimed with enthusiasm, handing him the reins.

Entering the house, Rosa sought out Calinta, who was doing some laundry. "Oh, Cally, it was so good to be out on the trails with Nightstar, again! It was a lovely day for a ride!"

Calinta's resolve to scold Rosa for being gone so long melted at the sight of her charge's radiant happiness. Instead, a bright smile broke across her face.

"Ride do Missy good. Make happy. Put stars in yo' eyes. Calinta have hot tea ready."

"Be back in a minute, Cally—I need to get out of this heavy clothing," Rosa answered, heading for her room. Removing her cape, she tossed it onto the bed and stood looking at her rosy-cheeked, starry-eyed image in the mirror.

"He said he loved me," she whispered aloud to herself.

Clasping her trembling hands tightly together over her heaving breast, the wonder of such a thought struck her at last. Always it had been John. There had been other boys in the area who had tried to catch her eye. One even tried to kiss her, but it had been John who remained constantly in her thoughts. Secretly, she had long hoped he would come to see her as more than just a friend.

Her face sobered as she recalled the last words of his confession of love. What did he mean that they were far apart in life? She saw no difference between a sailor and a farmer. Granted, her house was larger and probably more elaborate. She had no part in building it. Slaves? Where did he get the idea Calinta and Shonto were their slaves?

Returning to the warmth of the kitchen, she gratefully accepted the hot cup Calinta handed her, perching herself on the stool near the stove, usually occupied by Shonto. Cally came to offer her a tea cake, and Rosa studied her face.

"Cally, do you and Shonto consider yourselves to be our slaves?"

"Wi' fo' Missy ast?" Calinta queried abruptly, with widening eyes.

"Oh, some folks think we are better than they are because we live in a nice house and have slaves," answered Rosa, trying to be casual. However, she was not prepared for the change in Calinta's manner. A fierce expression came into her face as she stretched herself up proudly.

"Calinta, Shonto no slave!" she responded passionately. "Calinta, Shonto stay for' wha' feel in heah fo' Cap'n." She pointed to her heart. "Cap'n no pay. He say we free. We stay. Yo' family. Calinta, Shonto home!" She set the plate of cakes down and faced Rosa with a stern expression, hands on hips.

"Missy, no say slave, no day, no night."

"I'll never mention it again, Cally," promised Rosa, placing her cup on the table.

JOHN HAD STOOD ROOTED to the spot as Rosa turned her horse to ride quickly away, only to pull up short to wait for the lieutenant to catch up with her. He waved a farewell, but she did not respond. Her attention seemed to be on the handsome British soldier who rode by her side. Watching until they disappeared through the trees had left him with a nameless dread as questions crowded his mind.

Had he made a mistake taking her into his confidence? How long had she known this Lieutenant . . . Pennington? That's what she had called him. A terrible feeling he had never experienced before reared its ugly head. It gave him cause to wonder as he hurried home.

Thomas Giles was sitting on the porch putting on his work boots when John approached from the rear of the house to seat himself on the step. It was not unusual for his son to be out running the woods, so he offered no comment on his absence.

"Saw some Injun sign out north of here," John said quietly, looking out across the fields of drying corn.

Tom Giles paused, left boot in his hand, to peer from under a shaggy brow at his son. "That's the second time in as many days. Reckon they're after stealin' some stock?"

"Sure—it's hard to tell. They've been comin' in closer, though. Wished I knew. Anyone else losin' any stock?"

"Not that I know of. Well, I guess we'd better finish harvestin' the corn."

John followed his father to the field, where Tom continued the task of gathering the ears while John cut and stacked the corn stalks. Though he worked steadily, John found himself thinking of Rosa, thrilling at the picture of her face turned up to his and the light touch of her hand on his arm. What was it she was about to say when they were interrupted? Was she about to tell him there was someone else? Perhaps this Lieutenant Pennington? Reason told him no, but jealousy made him unsure.

All afternoon as he worked the battle raged within him. Hope was born in him again and again, only to be dashed by the fear of rejection. At the end of the day, when he stood by his father's side to survey the neat rows of corn stalks, he was not only physically weary but also heavyhearted and emotionally spent.

Supper was on the table when they trudged in from the fields, summoned by a couple of the younger children. Mary Giles, a slender woman with a tired face framed by brown hair streaked with gray, was happiest when her table was surrounded by her menfolk. One daughter, Martha, a child of 10, was her only help with household chores. John was her stepson, and it was to him she looked for assistance with the heavy work while her husband was away.

John was the last to get washed up and take his seat at the table. Hungry as he was, it was difficult to eat. His stomach still seemed tied into knots. He was grateful everyone at the table was too busy filling their own mouths to take note of the pretense he made at eating. Quietly listening to the never-ending banter of the good-natured group, he was not sure when the idea took fruition in his mind. Perhaps it came from a deep desire to see Rosa. But at that moment he determined, after all were in bed, he would slip away to see her.

What else he would say he didn't know, but at least he could tell her where they could meet tomorrow. With this settled in his mind, he was able to finish the food left on his plate.

The days were long on the farm, and soon the children were tucked into their beds and the adults retired to rest. John lay awake, fully dressed, until he heard his father's loud snores. Raising the bar on the window shutter, he slipped through to drop noiselessly to the ground. He pulled the window closed to keep out the cold air and then headed out to the road leading into Castine. His long stride took him swiftly over the familiar road for a way before leaving the beaten path to take a short cut through the forest. Aware of the risk he was taking, he kept his ears tuned to the sounds of the night creatures, stopping every now and then to listen intently.

The Jarden house was dark when he arrived. He stood pondering which window would be Rosa's, then stooped to pick up some pieces of gravel. He could only guess. He tossed a missile to one of the upper windows and waited, going on to another when there was no response.

Inside, Rosa was lying awake when she heard the sound of something hitting the windowpane. Clink! She bolted upright in bed. Clink! There it was again! Someone was trying to get her attention. But who? Father? Rosa slipped from beneath the covers, drew back the drapes, and looked out. She could make out the dim outline of a man's figure. Frightened, she stepped back. A tap on the window was followed by John's harsh whisper calling her name.

"Rosa, it's John!"

Rosa peered into the darkness to make sure, then motioned him to the front door. Pulling on her robe, she picked up her slippers and ran with pounding heart to let him in. The turn of the key in the lock made a slight sound, but she had no fear Calinta would hear it from her sleeping quarters in the back of the house off the kitchen. John stepped through the door she held open for him.

"I didn't know which window was yours. I tried several before I found you!"

"It's a good thing you didn't get Calinta's window," Rosa whispered, closing the door behind him. "Wait here."

She left him to shut the door that led into the other part of the house and closed the drapes before returning to light a lamp. This accomplished, she turned to find John staring at her. Little did she realize the picture she made in the lamplight with her golden hair cascading down her shoulders.

"You . . . you are so pretty," he stammered, expelling a deep breath.

"Surely you didn't come all the way at this late hour to tell me I'm pretty," she responded, smiling up at him.

"No, I didn't do that," he admitted honestly. "I came to see if you made it home without . . . uh, without further trouble." He paused as if something was weighing heavily on his mind, adding, "This lieutenant seems to know you pretty well."

Rosa gazed steadily at his troubled face, letting his last remark sink into her consciousness. Slowly, it dawned on her he had misunderstood her purpose in leaving him there so unceremoniously to ride off with Lieutenant Pennington. He was jealous! The thought pleased her, and she tried to explain.

"John, I have only known the lieutenant a few days. He was in charge of the troops who surrounded our home. When I demanded to be taken to the commandant, it was he who escorted me there and brought me back. He is a conceited, ambitious man who thinks any woman should fall at his feet. That makes him dangerous.

"I didn't know he would follow me today. I suspect he's been assigned to keep an eye on my activities. They may still think Father is out there somewhere, and I was riding out to meet him. Whatever the reason, I must play the game to protect you and your family."

John dropped his head, taken aback at her words, ashamed he had doubted her. Rosa stepped closer to look up into his eyes.

"There are ways other than weapons to fight, John," she said softly. "I shall have to fight my way."

"Rosa, I . . . ," he began in a strangled voice.

"It's all right, John. I understand."

Suddenly, her love broke its bounds and Rosa leaned her head against his chest. The odor of balsam mingled with woodsmoke was in the buckskin jacket he wore. It spoke of the many hours he spent outdoors. She felt him give a start and then his arms came up to gently push her away.

"Rosa, this is not good," he said in an unsteady voice. "It was a mistake for me to come here, but I had to know what you were about to say today."

Rosa looked up at him with shining eyes. "I love you, John," she confessed simply, bringing a happy expression to his face. "Always it has been you. I wanted you to know, for only God knows what will happen to us in the terrible times ahead."

"Rosa, I must go. It is enough to see you and know your love for me. Perhaps, someday, I can ask your father for your hand in marriage."

"Where shall I meet you tomorrow?" she asked tremulously, struggling for composure.

"You mustn't," he warned. "It is not safe for you to ride the trails around Castine anymore."

"Nonsense!" she protested. "What can possibly happen to me? Nightstar can outrun any horse or man."

"If you see them," John said dryly. "Rosa, I didn't want to tell—to frighten you, but I've been seein' Indian signs around the farm. I don't know what it means. It could be they're meetin' with the British to form an alliance. If that happens, my father says no one will be safe."

"Lieutenant Pennington told me it isn't safe for me to ride alone. He said there are Indians in the area," Rosa recalled. "I didn't believe him. I thought he was just trying to scare me."

"So he warned you there are Indians, huh?" mused John. He turned to open the door. "Whatever the case, don't ride out. I'll come here when I can."

"When will I see you again?"

"Soon. Now, blow out the lamp."

"Be careful, John," Rosa said softly, hastening to obey.

Closing the door quietly behind him, John paused momentarily to allow his vision to adjust to the moonless night, grateful for the cold air that fanned his cheeks and cooled his temples. He remained inert, searching the shadows around him.

The sound of an approaching horse made him drop to the floor and wiggle off the open porch to melt into the bushes. The rider stopped in front of the house. John could hear the creaking of leather as he shifted in the saddle. His heart was pounding so hard he was afraid it would give his presence away. But the horseman finally moved on down the road toward the harbor.

John stood to his feet, peering after the rider. Though he could not see well enough to identify the man, he knew in his mind it was Lieutenant Pennington. He would have to be more careful, he admitted grimly to himself. Starting toward home, he kept a fast pace, keeping to the shelter of the trees. Only when he entered the clearing of their farm did he slacken his gait.

Out front of the house a dog growled. It was Scoundrel. John could tell by the faithful dog's low guttural sound it wasn't directed at another animal. There was only one thing that could make Scoundrel act like that. Indians!

He hurried to his unlatched window and hoisted himself inside, dropping the bar in place. Then, he slipped on through the house to where his dad slept. His hand on his father's shoulder awakened the elder Giles instantly.

John tiptoed out to wait for him in the big room at the front of the house that served as a kitchen, dining area, and living room. A large fireplace, with a half-burned log, took up nearly one whole wall. Scoundrel's snarl had become more intense as he strained at his rope. When his father joined him, John whispered the one word they feared most. "Indians!"

Tom Giles took down the musket he kept over the fireplace and slung the powder horn over his shoulder. Outside, they heard Scoundrel give out a loud yelp, followed by silence. Their worried glances locked, and both knew the faithful animal had met a terrible fate.

John felt the hair stand up on the back of his neck when the elder Giles loaded his gun and stood with it aimed at the door. Searching for a weapon for himself, his eyes fell on the long knife his father used to cut the stalks of corn. He picked it up and held it steady. Forever etched in his memory would be his father's heavy breathing and fierce expression as they silently waited for what seemed an eternity.

Ever so slightly, the latch on the door moved, making a slight noise, as someone tried the lock. John heard a grunt, then the soft pad of a moccasined foot. Then all was quiet again.

"Check all the shutters and see if they have the bars across," ordered Tom in a hoarse whisper.

Moments later, John returned to assure his father all was secure and that the rest were asleep, unaware of the danger lurking a few feet away. Tom settled himself in a chair, and John followed suit. Hours passed without further incident, prompting the two of them to return to their beds for some much-needed sleep. John's last fleeting thought, before he faded into the unconsciousness of sleep, was Rosa's smiling face floating before him.

Rattling plates and the chatter of children's voices mingled with the smells of breakfast awakened him the next morning. Tired as he was, he threw back the covers and sat up to pull on his trousers. He wanted to look around outside before the children started moving about. It was then he remembered Scoundrel. He hurriedly slipped his feet into his shoes and picked up his jacket and hat.

"Well, you're getting up awfully late this morning," greeted Mary Giles, looking up from the meat she was frying.

"Where's Pa?" asked John, noting his father's absence.

"Still in the bed—must have worked too hard in the field yesterday," was her reply. Noting the jacket in his hands, she continued, "If you're going out, would you bring in a fresh pail of water?"

John put on his hat and coat, picked up the bucket, emptied the contents into the dishpan, and went out. The morning was blustery and cold, with a leadened sky. A stiff, icy wind was blowing out of the northeast, the harbinger of bad weather.

"There'll be snow before nightfall," he muttered, lowering the bucket into the well. Once it was filled, he took it to the house and placed it just inside the door. He would need to check the dog before one of the children caught sight of him.

Scoundrel had retreated as far as his rope had allowed. Had he been loose, he would have stood a better chance against his attacker. His inert body was on its side, with the head crushed by a single blow from the club of an Abenaki warrior.

This fierce tribe once freely roamed the area but now had been pushed farther north by the invasion of the settlers. They had always had a strong alliance to the French but had been known to join the British in several conquests.

John cut the rope and dragged the carcass out to the weeds behind the barn. Coming back around the barn, he carried some feed to the stock and returned to study the ground. There were moccasin prints in the dust where the dog was killed. The tracks leading to the porch told the chilling story. Had entrance been gained to the house, they would all be dead or suffering a worse fate.

Noting the direction of the tracks leading off toward the woods, he broke a branch from a nearby bush to erase the tracks and cover the blood.

With the telltale signs gone, John pondered the events of the last couple of days. To have the Indians this far south didn't make sense, unless the British anticipated an attack and had solicited their help. If this were true, why had their family been targeted? Had someone been informed of his father's allegiance to the Continental Army? Spies were everywhere; there could even be an informer among the men his father trusted.

His mind went to the encounter he had with the rider at Rosa's late last night. Was there a connection between the two incidents? Unable to fit the pieces together, John went in for breakfast. His father was up and sitting at the table. He gave him a quizzical look.

"Turnin' cold out there—I think we'll see some snow before nightfall," he announced, removing his coat and hat to hang them on a peg by the door.

Tom Giles looked at his tall, round-limbed, clear-eyed son warming his hands before the fire. He was the firstborn of his first wife, who was killed by the Indians as she was picking beans in the garden. A child of the wilderness, John had experienced at an early age the natural ability to hunt and track, moving through the forest glades instinctively with effortless, sure steps.

"Did you . . . uh, check the stock?"

"Took care of everything, Pa," replied John, sliding into his seat, "'cept milkin' the cow and bringin' the wood. I'll do that after breakfast. Shore Ma's gonna be needin' it."

Mary Giles flashed John a grateful smile as she brought him a plate of warm food.

"Better take the mule and stack up some more logs today," remarked John between mouthfuls. "Judgin' by all the signs I've seen, we're in for a cold one."

"You're probably right," the elder Giles responded, handing his cup to his wife. He had learned long ago not to question his son's aptitude for reading the weather. He retired to a chair by the fire to wait.

John ate heartily, knowing well it could be late before he would be eating again. He rose to his feet and reached for his coat. "Good breakfast, Ma," he said, looking out the one window on that side of the house while slipping his arms into the sleeves. Keen eyes searched every shrub and tree. A pair of red squirrels was frolicking along the ground under a big birch tree, a sure sign no Indian presence was in the area. Farther out, he spotted whitetail deer grazing. Picking up the milk bucket Mary Giles had readied, he headed for the barn.

He had just finished milking and was turning the cow out into the small barnyard when his father joined him.

"What do y' make of it, Son?"

John stared stoically off into the forest. It would be difficult to tell his father all that he knew or suspicioned without revealing he had been seeing Rosa. "I don't know for sure, Pa, but I have my 'spicions. I have no proof, but it 'pears like the British are expectin' an attack from our forces and have formed an alliance with the Abenakis. If this is true, we're in grave danger."

Tom Giles hit one fist into the other hand in a gesture of anger and exasperation. "Why, oh why hasn't General Lovell attacked by now?! From what I've been told, there's 1,500 men 'n' artillery commanded by Paul Revere just sittin' out there with a fleet of two dozen transports 'n' 19 heavily armed ships! That's not including the frigate *Warren* with all its 30 or more guns commanded by Captain Saltonstall." Tom Giles agonized explosively. "I don't know why they're waitin' for reinforcements. They've had enough men t' take Castine, and we would've helped if they weren't so yellow."

John knew what his father said was true. General Lovell and Captain Saltonstall had been too indecisive. But surely any day now more troops would arrive. He picked up the bucket of milk and took it into the kitchen and returned to chop wood. As he worked, an uneasiness crept over him. He tried to shake it off, but still it remained.

He straightened from his work to gaze into the forest, suddenly aware that a terrible quietness had settled down. Gone were the deer and the scampering squirrels. Birds that had been flitting from tree to tree were silent. No longer did he hear the call of the crow. He was about to call to his father, who was coming in from the wheat fields, when the sound of cannon fire came from the direction of the harbor. Gunfire echoed from the woods behind the house.

"They're here!" Tom Giles shouted, breaking into a run. "More troops have arrived. We're saved!"

But alas, he didn't see what John saw behind him. Abenaki warriors, with hideous painted faces, rose silently to their feet and began to advance toward them. John slowly backed toward the house. A blood-curdling yell split the air as he saw his father surrounded and dragged, fighting, to the ground.

Hearing the shouts, Mary Giles had run to the porch, followed by John's younger brothers and sister. A shot rang out, and she sank to the floor. Chaos ensued as John felt himself grabbed from behind and pushed down. Rough hands bound his arms and feet with leather thongs rendering him helpless. He watched in horror as his father was led to the yard, where he asked his captors if he could pray. He was allowed to sink to his knees and utter a prayer, then swiftly the club fell.

The cow and other livestock were led from the barn, disemboweled, and left to die a slow, painful death. An unnatural, fiendish glee surrounded the slaying of John's brothers. His sister, eyes glazed with terror, was being held captive by her long hair. Like him, she was being spared for some unknown reason.

John tried to call out to her but was promptly struck across the mouth and kicked. Indians swarmed through the house, looting, and setting fires. One warrior ran out brandishing his father's gun and powder horn. Another carried the long cutting knife John had left by the door. As the blaze spread throughout the dwelling, flames and thick black smoke shot high into the air.

The Indians were in no hurry to depart. One warrior sat on the ground contentedly eating a loaf of bread he had taken. Others squatted in a semicircle, watching the fire. They seemed in no fear of attack, leaving John to wonder: If reinforcements had indeed come, where were the soldiers who could have helped them? Even the cannon fire had ceased quickly. Had something gone wrong?

Snow began to fall. The first, big, wet flakes of the season slowly covered the grotesque scene with a mantle of white.

The house had been reduced to smoldering ruins before his captors removed the bindings from John's legs and prodded him to his feet with a long, sharp stick. Sickened to the core of his being, he took one last, long look at the mutilated bodies lying in the snow. Suddenly it struck him: one brother was missing. Hope sprang alive in his heart that the boy had somehow fled the fate of the others.

His sister, Martha, was nowhere to be seen, and when he turned his head to look for her, he was rewarded with a blow to the face by the fierce-looking warrior who goaded him into a run. The pace was held for hours, going north. Familiar landscapes were left behind as they pressed on. Ahead in the distance was a high peak. John etched it in his memory as a landmark to help him in his escape—and escape he would, if given the chance.

The snow was falling more heavily now, making the ground slippery. His fleet-footed captors appeared not to notice, continuing their steady gait. John found it awkward to keep his balance in the rough terrain with his arms tied to his sides, but he did his best to keep up. Gruesome stories came to mind of how others before him had been left behind, clubbed to death.

His thoughts turned to Rosa, and a haze came across his eyes. What would she think when he failed to come tonight? He was saddened by the fact it would be a long time before he would see her again—perhaps never. Would she wait for him? He determined he must live, no matter the cost, to come back to her.

The ground beneath him became a blur, and John did not see the log that tripped him. He fell to his knees, plunging face forward in the snow. The big Indian beat him across the back with the stick until John struggled to his feet to stagger on. The foremost runners had not slackened their momentum, forcing him to run faster to catch up. Thigh muscles burned with fatigue, and his breath, coming in short gasps, was like knife blades in his lungs. How much longer he could keep going he did not know. Yet he was not without admiration for these sons of the wilderness, who ran as deer through the rough terrain, jumping creeks and fallen trees.

The image of his father kneeling to pray for him in the last moments of his life gave John courage. "Dear God, please help me," he cried inwardly. "I want so much to live!" New strength flowed into him. Raising his head to the sky, he let out a strange, piercing cry of triumph, startling his kidnappers. They recovered, laughing among themselves, gesturing and pointing at John.

"Sannup! Sannup!" they shrieked in glee.

That one Abenaki word John knew. He had heard mothers call their sons "Little Sannup," the Abenaki word for warrior.

Dusk found them skirting a lake to their left, and a short way beyond they entered a thick grove of trees where the ground was still bare. Several of the braves dropped to the ground, while others gathered wood and built a fire. John's feet were tied again, and he was ignored. Glad for the opportunity to rest, he huddled in the cold, wet and miserable, sensing his presence was not welcome in their circle around the fire. After appeasing their hunger with food they had stolen from his home, they cut boughs from the trees to cover their bodies while they slept.

The stalwart warrior who had been in charge of him came toward him, arms ladened with limbs. Grunting something John didn't understand, the Indian pushed him down to the ground and covered him, leaving John to believe that though these seemed like bloodthirsty savages, they were not totally without compassion. Or, he reasoned silently, was he just taking care of his property as one would care for his livestock? Whatever the case, he was grateful for the protection from the cold wind. Had it not been for his bonds, he would almost be comfortable. Sleep came easily to his tired body.

Days later, John was pushed ahead of his captors across a narrow creek, near their village. The squaws and children came running out to meet them, staring curiously at him. The Indian who had led him through the wilderness said something to several of the women. John could only guess at what was taking place as the women nodded with a smile. They picked up sticks and started beating and poking him toward a shelter in the center of the camp. There he was tied to a stake.

LIEUTENANT PENNINGTON kept his eyes on Rosa as she rode up the hill toward her home, waiting until she turned in the yard out of sight. Then, turning his horse, he headed back the way they had just come. He wanted to take a look around the place where he had spotted her horse. Something about the whole episode did not ring true. Miss Jarden seemed very anxious to get him away from there.

Cautiously, he dismounted and tied his horse outside the small, shady glen. He drew his gun and walked forward slowly, his boots making but a slight sound in the pine needles. In the soft dirt, he could see his horse's hoof prints, along with those of the black mare that Miss Jarden had been riding.

He stopped to study the ground all around the opening into the rocks. He could see the imprint of the woman's soft boot as she had dismounted. Her footprints led into the rocks. There were other slight impressions that puzzled him. They looked as if they were made by a moccasin, usually worn by the Indians. Surely she would not be meeting an Indian out here alone, unless her father had sent a runner with a message.

Within that stronghold of rocks lay the answer. Should he risk entering that narrow entrance? If someone was hiding in there, he would certainly be at a disadvantage. Should it be Captain Jarden, he had no desire to fall into his hands.

Pennington crept stealthily to the entrance, where he listened intently. No sound other than the wind in the trees could be detected. With the hair on the back of his neck standing on end, he moved inward, hesitating with every step, straining his senses to catch the least movement. Perspiration formed on his brow as he flattened himself against the last boulder. At his foot was a large pebble. He kicked it to the inside. There was no response. Cautiously, he edged in.

It was certainly a private place for one to hide, but he saw no evidence of a private moment, as Miss Jarden had put it. He could see her footprints all over the place and the same indentations that were on the outside. He stared at the ground with a frown. Then it dawned on him. Those slight dents were made by someone wearing soft deerskin boots, who walked with the light step of an Indian—probably a white man, since there were none of the usual Indian signs. Probably not her father—he was too heavy. But who?

Returning to the area outside, he walked in a wide circle until he picked up the slight prints heading out in the direction of the Giles' farm. He trailed for a short distance to make sure, then doubled back to his horse. So that was it! "Miss High and Mighty" was meeting that Tom Giles pup. What was his name? John? Yes, that was it. He had seen him around. He wore deerskin boots!

Well, that won't last long, he thought darkly as he stepped into the saddle and headed for town. He had long known about Tom Giles' sympathy for the Revolutionaries. And now, through his spy, he had positive proof of his activities against the British forces.

Tonight he was to meet with a delegation of the Indian confederacy to plan an end to the Giles' influence in the area. After Giles was destroyed, he would set them on the trail of all those who were involved. That should hold down any insurrection for a while. With the fort nearly finished, they should be able to withstand any invading force until help arrived.

Pleased with the way matters were shaping up, Howland

Pennington turned his thoughts to Rosa Jarden. How much was she involved in all this? It was true that her father, Captain Jarden, was said to be engaged in providing supplies to the Continental Army, a fact she denied knowing about. Well, that was of no consequence. What could a slip of a woman do anyway? He could handle her. Before his mission was completed, she would be glad for his presence. A sardonic smile came to his lips, and a strange fire burned in his dark, brooding eyes at the thought.

Glancing up at the sun, Pennington determined he would need to hurry. There would be just enough daylight left to have something to eat at the tavern before riding out at dusk. He spurred his horse into a gallop, choosing the trail that ran along the high bluff overlooking the harbor. A heavy fog was hanging offshore like a gray wall. He could only hope it remained so. Finding his way through the woods in a fog was not something he relished.

He turned his horse onto the main road leading up to headquarters, unaware that Captain Mowatt was watching his approach. Dismounting in front of the building, he was in the act of securing the reins when Corporal Beasley appeared to inform him the captain wished to see him. Casting a hungry glance toward the tavern, he followed the corporal inside.

"Where have you been, Lieutenant?" was the greeting.

"Out on surveillance, sir."

"Find anything interesting?"

"Just confirming what you already knew to be true, sir: The Giles family is guilty of working against the crown," replied Lieutenant Pennington, choosing not to reveal what he had learned about Miss Jarden.

"You'll be riding out to meet with our Indian allies soon, eh? Their raid should put an abrupt end to the activities of Tom Giles and others like him. If we are attacked from the sea, at least we won't have to worry about someone firing at our backsides. Just make sure there are no slip-ups. Corporal Beasley will have the bounty pouch ready." Captain Mowatt settled back in his chair, fixing his stern gaze on his righthand man, who seemed hesitant. "Was there something else?"

"It's just that I thought I would stop over at the tavern for something to eat before leaving out."

"See to it—you know the time you need to get out there," replied Captain Mowatt in dismissal.

Lieutenant Pennington spun on his heels and hurried down the hall, leaving his commander to stare at the empty doorway.

Captain Mowatt stood to his feet with furrowed brow. Stepping into the hall, he stroked his chin thoughtfully as he watched his lieutenant leave the building. Long years in the service of the British army had taught him many things. One was to doubt the motives of his men when they were not exactly truthful with him.

Lieutenant Pennington's evasive reply raised a question in his mind. Ambitious and eager, the lieutenant was above reproach in his service record, carrying out orders in the most precise manner. But there was something about the man that bothered Captain Mowatt at times—something he could not quite put his finger on.

Shaking his head, he picked up his hat and went to his quarters. Maybe he had been in this God-forsaken land too long, he thought gloomily. Hanging his hat on a peg on the wall, he picked up a picture of his wife he kept on a stand near his bed. It had been almost a year since he had seen her and held her in his arms. The English countryside where they lived seemed so far away at this moment. He sank down onto the bed, tired and weary of it all. This would be his last command.

A glimmer of light through the trees caused Howland Pennington to bring his horse to a halt. Never comfortable in a situation of this kind, he dreaded this meeting. All too well, he knew there was nothing to prevent these wild creatures from simply taking his life and the bounty. What could one do among so many? Yet had he not built up a trust with these Indians? He spurred his horse forward to enter firelight.

The Indians sat in a semicircle and, as usual, gave no heed to his presence among them. He had grown used to that, knowing he must be seated and wait for them to make the first overture. Because of their long association with the French, they spoke to him in that language.

What a strange, wild setting! His companions sat immobile, dark gleaming eyes staring into the fire. Flickering flames played over their stoic countenances. The slightest sound to his back reminded him there were other eyes watching from the cover of the night.

When the talk finally began, he was quick to state his purpose for soliciting their aid. He drew a map in the dirt, indicating the location of the Giles farm and the others.

Madowock, a stalwart fellow wearing several feathers in his warlock, grunted with satisfaction. He turned and said something in their native tongue to the warrior on his right. The man grunted, his eyes narrowing perceptibly as he looked over at Howland Pennington.

Lieutenant Pennington gave no indication of noticing this little byplay, but went on drawing the number of people in the family. Then he drew a line that beheaded them all.

"Before the sun sets again," he said, speaking fluent French.

"It will be as you say, Penn-ing-ton," replied the leader, rising to his feet.

The time for talk was over abruptly. Lieutenant Pennington went to his horse and brought back the bounty Corporal Beasley had put together. He laid it on the ground beside the fire, where it was pounced on immediately in search of "firewater."

Pennington stepped into his saddle and slowly rode away without looking back. To look back would have been a sign of weakness and cowardice. Whoops and shrieks gave evidence they had found what they were seeking. Before this night was over, death would stalk the wooded aisles of the forest. Once he had gone a safe distance, he slapped his horse into a fast trot, increasing his speed when he turned into the familiar trail leading past the fort.

Coming down the main street in Castine, his horse moved noiselessly in the sand. As he neared the Jarden house, he thought he saw a pinpoint of light, but it was gone so suddenly he was not sure. It had been a long day. Was that a shadow? He brought his horse to a halt and sat there for a moment wondering what to do. Should he investigate?

He listened for a moment, eyes trying to penetrate the darkness surrounding the house. Shifting his weight in the saddle, he decided not to pursue the matter. If it was John Giles, he would soon be but a passing memory. Captain Jarden was another matter, but there would be a time for his demise. Releasing his tight hold on the reins, he gave his mount its head and rode on down the street with the uncomfortable feeling someone was watching him depart.

Indeed, there were two sets of eyes watching him ride away. Rosa had run to the darkened window in time to see John drop quickly to the floor and crawl into the shadows. Looking to see what had precipitated this behavior, she spotted a rider coming into view. Rosa had to clamp her hand over her mouth to keep from crying out when she recognized the rider was Howland Pennington. What was he doing out so late at night? Had he been spying on her? Had he seen John leave the house? Standing there gazing out at him, she felt as if he were reading her thoughts. She retreated farther into the room, fearful he could hear the pounding of her heart.

After an indefinable length of time, he rode on down the street. Rosa ran to the side window in time to see a dark silhouette rise out of the hedge and flee. Without a doubt, John had escaped discovery, simply because the lieutenant decided not to intervene in the matter. This puzzled her. Expelling a long, deep sigh brought her to the realization she had been holding her breath. Trembling from head to toe, she sought her bed.

Though she had spent many sleepless hours, Rosa was up

early to face a gray, dismal day. A cold wind had come up, and low-hanging clouds were moving in from the west. Gratefully, she accepted the hot cup of tea Calinta offered her. She sat whitefaced and hollow-eyed, sipping it quietly, lost in thought, unaware of the worried glance Calinta cast her way. Shonto came in to perch himself in his usual place by the fire.

"Missy Rosa, Nightstar wanna run. She feel good! Missy gon' ride?"

"No, Shonto, I don't think so," answered Rosa, slowly. "The weather looks bad, and besides, I've been told it isn't safe." She turned to Calinta. "There's Indian activity in the area. Shonto should not be straying far from the house."

"Who say Indian here?" asked Calinta, her hand going to a fetish hanging around her neck.

"Father, for one, and Lieutenant Pennington." Rosa did not wish to mention what John had told her.

"Shonto see Injun, Shonto run fast," boasted the boy, with a big, white-toothed smile, his eyes bright.

"Shonto, be careful," exclaimed Rosa, gazing at the strange little bag Calinta was wearing as a necklace. "Cally, what is that you're wearing?"

"It medicine bag. Make evil spirits go away!"

"Cally," scoffed Rosa, "there are no evil spirits here—just people! You don't need that here among friends."

"Missy Rosa, Calinta know de' spirits—I can feel 'em all round dis' lan'—dey's gwine sneakin' here and dere," was the forceful reply, as Calinta faced Rosa with troubled eyes rolling in her head. "Sumpin' bad gon' happen. Calinta see!"

In all her years, Rosa had never seen Calinta so troubled or upset. The woman's face was a study of fear as she began to sway back and forth, moaning. She looked over at Shonto, who sat transfixed while watching his aunt.

"Shonto, you don't believe what she's saying, do you?"

"Missy Rosa, I don' see dis a'fore—wh' fo' she talk like dis?" answered the boy, keeping his gaze on the swaying woman.

"Well, I don't believe in your witchcraft!" Rosa said emphatically, hitting the table with her hand. "I have been taught to trust a providential God. He will take care of us! He is the Great Spirit, and He is in control. Do you hear me? Now stop that carrying on!"

Breakfast was finished without further incident. Shonto and Calinta conversed in low tones in their native language while Rosa lingered over a last cup of tea.

Suddenly a loud explosion split the stillness of the peaceful morning air, followed by smaller cannon fire. Rosa, Calinta, and Shonto looked from one to the other with stunned silence. It seemed to be coming from the harbor! Rosa ran to the front of the house to look out the window facing the water.

Several ships bearing the British flag had entered the harbor and were firing their guns at an unseen enemy. Rosa knew they had surprised and were in pursuit of the American ships that had been hiding there for days. Trapped in the Penobscot River with no escape to the open sea, the Continental forces would have no way of escape.

Her heart sank as she comprehended what it was going to mean to all who longed for deliverance. Their hope for freedom was disappearing with each shot. Poor John—this would be a crushing blow.

Rifle fire could be heard off in the distance, north of town. British troops were pouring into the streets, heading for the fort and out toward the bluff. Giving over the view from that window to Calinta and Shonto, who had joined her, Rosa ran upstairs to her father's room to look out toward the fort. No one there seemed to be responding with gunfire. It was coming from farther away. From where she stood, she could see black smoke billowing above the treetops. Paralyzing fear gripped her, causing the blood to leave her face as she realized it was in the direction of the Giles' farm. "John! Oh, dear God!" she whispered.

"Cally, Shonto, come here—hurry!"

When they had joined her, she cried, "Look—see that

smoke? I think there's a fire at the Giles' farm. What should we do?"

"Missy, dey's no ting we do. Bad . . . bad," Cally groaned, stroking the fetish at her neck.

Rosa stood with tears trickling down her cheeks. Of course, Cally was right. What could they do but watch and hope? The silence was unbroken as they remained there until the fire had died out of sight behind the trees. Calinta led the distraught girl down the stairs to the warmth of the kitchen and seated her at the table.

"Missy, yo' be good. Calinta 'n' Shonto hep yo'," she crooned. "No ting bad come t' yo' . . ."

A knock at the front door interrupted her. Patting Rosa on the shoulder, Calinta went to answer. Rosa heard a man's voice and Calinta's soft answer, both indistinct, followed by footsteps in the hall.

Rosa quickly wiped the tears from her face, casting a warning glance at Shonto, who positioned himself near the door leading into the stables. Picking up her teacup, she sipped the cold tea, trying to give the appearance of calm as she sat with her back to them.

"Missy Rosa, I don tole' him yo' no see him," Calinta sputtered, anxiously beating the air with her hands.

"I assured her you would want to see me," said Lieutenant Pennington, confidently. "I came to see if you are all right after the skirmish that took place this morning." He stopped, waiting for a reply; when none came, he went on.

"Our reinforcements arrived and overcame the insurrection. You will be able to live in peace. Of course, we British will take care of those who are loyal to the crown."

Rosa spun around. In there somewhere was a veiled threat. The arrogance of this man! He stood there smiling at her, handsome as ever in his impeccable uniform.

"Thank you, Lieutenant," she responded coldly. "It is good to know you will leave us alone to live in peace."

He stiffened ever so slightly at her rebuff, then relaxed

again, smiling down at her. She watched, fascinated, at the tiny pinpoints of light appearing in his dark eyes. His bold glance caressed her face, bringing heightened color.

"Calinta, the lieutenant is leaving—please show him to the door," Rosa said, tearing her eyes away.

"That's all right, Calinta. I know the way." He moved toward the kitchen door, placing his hand on the doorknob. "Oh, by the way," he said dispassionately, as if it had just occurred to him, "you shouldn't be riding much for a while unless accompanied by someone. It is very dangerous. The Indians attacked the Giles family and several others. There were no survivors." He paused. "Perhaps you saw the smoke. I have ordered a detail out to bury the bodies. Good day."

His words hit her heart like bullets fired from a gun. Rosa felt the blood leave her face, and she gripped the table where she was sitting. In the stunned silence that followed, his retreating footsteps sounded like a hammer against an anvil. The room reeled before her, and she heard Calinta calling her name as blackness engulfed her.

6

SEVERAL DAYS PASSED before Rosa felt like resuming classes with Calinta and Shonto. It was as much for her own welfare as theirs. She had to keep her mind occupied to keep her sanity. None of them mentioned the tragedy, but Rosa noticed that Calinta and Shonto were more than attentive to her every need. The snow had continued with large, wet flakes swirling down, bearing heavily on the branches of the shrubs and trees.

Looking out the window from where she sat reading, Rosa could not see more than a hundred feet. Only the hardy and the soldiers ventured out into the cold, white world. Rosa felt isolated, lonely. Father! Where was he? Finding it hard to concentrate any longer, she laid her book aside. Shonto came in with an armload of wood for her fire. Since there were still several pieces lying in the box, she suspected it was a ruse to check on her.

"Shonto, how is Nightstar doing?" asked Rosa, surprised that she had forgotten about the mare.

"Oh, Missy, 'at Nightstar doin' good," responded the boy.

Rosa watched as he stacked the wood neatly in the box and stoked the fire. Wise beyond his years, Shonto was adept at many things. Slender and strong as a willow, he had a grace of movement that seemed in harmony with everything around him. She didn't even know his age.

"Shonto, how old are you?" she asked, curiously.

"Old? Shonto not old. Shonto young." He grinned, showing a wide row of white teeth. His eyes showed his pleasure at her interest.

"What's Cally doing?" asked Rosa, changing the subject.

"She . . . how you say? Cooking?"

"Whatever it is, it smells good!" she laughed, jumping to her feet. "Come—let's go and see."

"Cally," she sang out, "what smells so good? Mmmmmm."

"'at Lootenent dun giv' us a big bird he killed in de' woods," answered Calinta, beaming at the change in Rosa.

Rosa's smile vanished. The nerve of him! First they confiscate most of the supplies—then he expects them to accept charity. Well, they would just send it back. They could get by without his handouts. She did not wish to be indebted to the man.

Calinta had pulled the pan out of the oven for her to see, smiling proudly. It was a big turkey. Shonto stood hungrily eyeing the meat, which filled the kitchen with a delicious aroma. Rosa found herself licking her lips. Well, just this once, but no more. If she sent it back now, it wouldn't be fair to them. Whom was she fooling? She was as hungry for meat as they were.

"It's beautiful, Cally!" she exclaimed instead. "We'll have to use it sparingly and make it last for a long time, though. I don't wish to accept that man's charity. I don't think it's good to be beholden to him."

Calinta nodded her agreement, basting the bird before pushing it back into the oven.

"Shonto, I'll get my cape and we'll go see Nightstar," said Rosa, heading for her room.

She returned to find Shonto waiting by the door leading into the stable area. Today, with the weather so bad, she was grateful her father had built his home like those of many of the other people who lived in the area. Out of necessity, those who settled the land had constructed their outbuildings connected to the main house. One could venture out in severe weather and become lost just yards from safety. So it was a practical idea to be able to go through the woodshed, where the tools were kept, into the barn, where the animals were sheltered. Hay was stored overhead.

Nightstar heard her voice and whinnied a greeting, her proud head stretched to receive a treat Rosa always carried. Her warm, velvety nose searched Rosa's outstretched hand.

"I declare, Nightstar—I often wonder what you would do if I didn't bring you something," she laughed, looking over at Shonto, who had his head cocked as if listening.

"What is it, Shonto?" she asked.

He held his hand up in a warning sign and crept nearer the door going to the outside. The knob was turning slightly, then stopped. There was a thumping sound; then all was silent. The two stared at each other, wondering what to do. Should they risk opening the door?

Shonto picked up a pitchfork and stood listening. There was no further sound from the other side of the door.

"Missy, yo' stand back."

Rosa backed into the shadows as Shonto reached for the bar across the door and lifted it. The door swung open, revealing a snow-covered heap just outside. Large footprints led off toward the woods. Shonto looked both ways, then, satisfied no one was lurking nearby, laid the pitchfork aside and motioned for Rosa to help him. He brushed the snow away, revealing a girl's face, white as death.

"Martha Giles!" gasped Rosa, peering over his shoulder. "Hurry, Shonto—let's get her in from the cold. Poor dear! I wonder how she got here."

Shonto pointed to the mysterious bootprints in the snow. Quickly, they dragged the girl inside and barred the door. She moaned slightly.

"She's still alive, Shonto! Go get Cally. Hurry! We need to get her in where it's warm."

While she waited, Rosa removed her warm cape and

wrapped it around the girl, clad in tattered clothing, and an Indian buckskin jacket that had seen its best days. Shonto and Calinta came running. They carefully lifted the frail body and carried her into the house.

"Put her in my room—no one will discover her there, and besides, she'll need care night and day," instructed Rosa.

"Shonto, fix fire; Calinta bring warm water; Missy, make clean; Calinta make soup," the African woman said in a quiet, take-charge manner, as they deposited the nearly frozen child onto the bed.

While Rosa waited for Calinta to return with the water, she brushed the hair, matted with mud and debris, away from Martha's brow. How still and white she was! Her face was full of angry-looking scratches, and dirt was caked under the torn and bloody nails of her fingers, evidence that she had dragged herself along the ground.

Calinta returned with the water, and Shonto discreetly left the room. It was no small task to bathe the unconscious girl, but soon she was warm and comfortable in one of Rosa's gowns.

How far had she come today? Some compassionate soul had found her and brought her here, knowing she would be safe and cared for—someone who didn't wish to be seen. Even in her wildest imagination, Rosa could not guess who it could be.

Just then a revelation of truth flashed into her mind! If Martha was alive, could it be there were other survivors? Perhaps John? Hope sprang anew in her heart. "Please, dear God, let it be so," she whispered.

Calinta came with the soup, and Rosa gave over the care and feeding to her expert hands. Shonto entered to stir up the fire, adding wood. He remained to watch at a respectful distance. It was difficult to get more than a few drops down the girl at a time, but Calinta patiently kept at it.

"No mo'," she said, finally, setting the cup aside. "Mo afta while. We eat now. Missy eat here."

Rosa drew up a chair by the bedside to wait for Calinta to bring her a tray. She noted a little color was beginning to return to Martha's face. Her hands moved restlessly beneath the covers.

The long afternoon hours passed slowly as the three kept their vigil, giving intermittent feedings and tending to the needs of their patient. Outside, the snowstorm continued to rage, showing little sign of letting up. The drifting snow was up to the window ledges, pushed there by the fierce wind.

Darkness would come early with the heavy overcast. While Rosa sat with Martha, Calinta and Shonto prepared the lamps, filling them with oil, trimming the wicks, and cleaning the globes. When lit, their golden glow added to the warmth of the room.

"Cally, we'll keep the drapes closed to keep anyone from spying on us," Rosa instructed, pulling them over the window. "Not that man or beast would want to be out on a night like this," she added. "But one never knows to what lengths some people will go.

"And another thing. No one must know Martha Giles is here with us, understand? No one." Rosa paused to make sure they grasped the importance of what she was saying. "The lieutenant has probably heard by this time . . ."

A piercing scream from the bed interrupted her, startling them all. With eyes fixed in terror, Martha had raised up in the bed and was beating the air with her arms, as if to fight off an unseen assailant. Rosa and Calinta ran to quiet the wild-eyed girl, who fought like a tiger.

"No! No!" she shrieked. "Stay away from me! Stay away, I say! Let me go! John! Where are you? Help me! John, don't leave me here! Johnnnnn!"

It took all the strength they could muster to hold the horror-stricken girl as she raved, trying to bite them. Finally, Calinta released her hand and gave the girl a resounding slap across the face. Rosa was both surprised and shocked at her action, but the girl went limp and began to whimper. Realizing

Calinta meant it for good, Rosa began to talk to the child, trying to quiet her.

"Martha, listen to me! Martha, it's Rosa!" She held her by the shoulders, forcing her to lay back. "Do you hear me? It's Rosa. You are here with me. You are safe. We are going to take care of you. Shhhh. Be quiet. You are safe here." Rosa cradled the girl's head in her arms, crooning and reassuring her until she had grown still. Gradually, the fear left Martha's eyes, and she gazed intently at Rosa until she fell asleep again.

"What terrible things she must have seen and been through, Cally!" Rosa agonized, looking over her head at Calinta. "We must watch her carefully until we are sure she is herself, or she may try to run away."

All during the night they took turns watching the fretful girl, who began running a fever. Her face became flushed and hot. Her speech was incoherent and rambling, calling first for her mother and then for John. Sometimes she would laugh. Cold cloths were kept on her forehead, in an attempt to keep the fever in check.

For three days they fought the battle against pneumonia. There were times when it seemed the girl would not make it. On the morning of the fourth day the fever broke, and she lay weakened and drenched with perspiration. When she opened her sad, gray eyes to gaze around the room, Rosa could tell a difference. The terror was gone.

"She's better, Cally. I can tell by her eyes.

"Martha, it's Rosa. You're safe here with me. We'll take care of you."

The girl tried to frame a word, but she was too weak to talk.

"Don't try to talk now. There's time for that later. Cally wants to feed you some soup. You must try to eat. It will give you strength."

All the while Calinta was feeding her, Martha's eyes did not leave Rosa's face. When Calinta had finished and had taken the bowl away, Rosa was arranging Martha's pillow when she was surprised to hear Martha whisper John's name. What was the girl trying to tell her? Dare she ask? Cally and Shonto were both in the kitchen.

"What about John, Martha?" asked Rosa, leaning close.

The girl did not answer right away but continued to look at Rosa.

"Where is John?" urged Rosa, holding her breath.

A puzzled expression came across Martha's solemn face as she struggled to remember. Her somber gaze turned toward the window with a faraway look. Of course, Rosa thought, if John had escaped or had been taken captive by the Indians, the girl would not know his whereabouts. She changed her question.

"Martha, is John alive?"

The sad face lit up a little, and something akin to gladness came alive for an instant in the sad eyes. The lips formed a silent "Yes."

"Oh, Martha, John will come back to us—we'll wait for him," cried Rosa softly, embracing her. "You must get well."

Martha averted her face, refusing to look at her. Rosa saw tears spill down her cheeks onto the pillow. She drew Martha close to her, holding her until she fell asleep. Slipping away, she found her chair by the fire, glad for the time alone to think. John was alive! This knowledge lifted her spirits.

Her mind went back to that fateful night he had come to the house. Reliving those moments that seemed so long ago, Rosa remembered the comforting warmth of his nearness. Both young and in love, they were caught in the perils of a war-torn, fledgling nation, fighting for its freedom from tyranny. Now, knowing there was a good chance John was alive, she determined the strength of her love and prayers would bring him back to her. Could he hear her heart crying out for him?

Shonto came in to check on the fire, followed moments later by Calinta, who peered closely at the sleeping Martha. Rosa left the room and wandered into the front parlor, as if somehow drawn there to recapture a sense of John's presence. Standing where they had held each other, her heart cried out to him. She fell to her knees, hands pressed against her mouth.

Everyone dear to her had been taken away. A moan escaped her lips as a great longing for comfort and strength assailed her. Sobs racked her body; her grief overwhelmed her. It seemed her heart would break.

From the time she was a small child she had been taught to consider God's providence and care. The Bible, which had been so much a part of her mother's life, had been read and quoted. Had she not been raised in a religious atmosphere? Yet in her heart, Rosa sensed there should be more.

Calinta heard Rosa's cry and, leaving Martha in Shonto's care, came to see about her. The weeping Rosa did not hear the light step behind her.

"Missy, wh' fo' yo' hurtin' so, Babee?" cried a concerned Calinta, bending over her.

"Oh, Cally, I . . . I miss them so," sobbed Rosa. "Mother, then Father, and now John. He . . . he was . . . all I . . . had left. It seems . . . everything I've held dear is gone, but you and Shonto."

Calinta knelt to gather the heartbroken girl into her arms. Like herself, Rosa had been subjected to a lot for one person to handle in a short lifetime.

Cradling Rosa in her lap, Calinta stroked the golden head. "Mama, gone. Cap'n—he come back; yo' see. John?"

"John Giles, Cally. I love him," confessed Rosa, looking through her tears into the sympathetic black face.

"It hurts me here." Rosa placed her hands over her heart.

"Missy hurt—Calinta know. My man down wi' ship," the African woman confided, drying Rosa's tears with the corner of her apron. "Wh' fo' yo' God too little? Yo' tell Calinta 'n' Shonto, yo' God biiiig God," she went on a little sharply, waving her arms in a wide circle. "Yo' say yo' God see wh' eyes, hear wh' ears, do anythin'. Yo' say talk wh' God, He talk wh' yo.'"

Stung by her rebuke, Rosa pushed herself up to a sitting position. Calinta was right. She had been teaching them about a God she knew only as a providential Caretaker. She met Calinta's keen glance with a frank, troubled gaze.

"You're right, Cally," she said, soberly. "I've known about God here," Rosa continued, pointing to her head, "but I haven't really known Him here." She placed her hand over her heart, feeling very small and humbled.

Days passed without incident, and though Martha continued to gain strength, she still remained aloof and withdrawn. Rosa kept trying to draw her into the daily activities, but it was difficult to get the girl to remain at anything very long. She would often find her sitting idle, staring out the window.

Milder weather followed the terrible storm that struck the area, melting most of the early snow. Long icicles hung from the eaves of the house. Rosa was reading to her audience of three when they heard heavy footsteps on the side porch.

They stared at one another in alarm at a heavy knock on the door. Rosa closed her book and told Shonto to hurry with Martha to the bedroom. Rosa followed Calinta into the kitchen, staying in the background. Calinta opened the door to find a barrelchested man of medium build standing there. He was dressed in the usual garb of a sea captain, and it was obvious he was nervous about being there. His clear blue eyes framed by a shock of unruly red hair darted over his shoulders to see if he was being observed.

"Is this the residence of Miss Rosa Jarden?" he inquired in a deep voice.

Calinta turned to give Rosa a questioning look.

"It's all right, Cally—I'll take care of it," Rosa said, stepping into the light. "Yes, I am Rosa Jarden."

"Good day, miss; may I come in?" he said gruffly, glancing back over his shoulder.

"Please do." Rosa stepped back to allow him to enter, closing the door behind him.

"Would you like some hot tea?"

"Thank you, but there's no time—I came at great risk to bring you this," he said, pulling a rumpled letter from his pocket. "I must be on my way."

"You may leave through the stables and go out the back

way, if you wish," Rosa instructed, taking the letter. "Cally will show you. And, Captain, God go with you."

He followed Calinta to the stable door, where he paused. "Your father saved my life; I owed it to him," he informed her with a warm smile. "I'll be telling him you are well. Good-bye."

Rosa stared at the door where he had disappeared, trying to comprehend what he had just said. He would be seeing her father! That meant he was alive, somewhere. With a trembling hand, she opened the letter. It was written in her father's hand.

My Dear Rosa,

This letter comes to let you know I am well. Since I last saw you, I escaped the net the British had set for me, but I was attacked by pirates and made captive. Alas, Caleb, your friend and mine, was run through with a sword. It brings sadness to my heart to tell you this, as it will yours, but I knew you would want to know. Things are better now. The pirate ship was boarded by an American frigate, and I was released. I have been assigned a new ship by a wealthy merchant. I had hoped to be home in time to share Christmas with you. My heart will be there, though I dare not. There are things afoot that will soon mean freedom for us all. Until then, I trust God's providence to keep you safe. Give my regards to Calinta and Shonto. Happy Christmas to you all.

Affectionately yours,
Father

Rosa held the letter to her heart, her face radiant with joy. "He's alive, Cally—Father's alive!" she rejoiced when Calinta returned. "Oh, thank God! He has answered our prayers!"

"Cally say Cap'n 'live," said Calinta, feeling for her fetish with a wry smile. "Cally know Cap'n be good."

"Cap'n be all right," corrected Rosa, undaunted by the reference Cally made to her native beliefs. "Come—we'll go tell the others, and I'll read you his letter."

That night in bed, Rosa found herself too excited to sleep. Relieved to know her father was alive and well, she lay there thinking, watching the flickering patterns the firelight made on the ceiling. In his letter, her father had given reference to something about to occur that would mean freedom from British rule. If only it would happen soon!

She knew without asking that their rations were getting low. Cally had used the last of the few pieces of turkey to make soup that very day. The last of the flour was in the larder. Now that the tea was low, they had resorted to drinking hot water, except for breakfast. The lamps had the last of the oil in them. Starting tomorrow, they would begin using them sparingly, depending more on the fire to provide light as well as heat. Shonto had assured her they had enough wood for a while.

Heaving a great sigh, Rosa looked over at the sleeping girl. Caring for the three people in her home laid a heavy responsibility on her. Now there were four mouths to feed.

Looking back over the last two months, she thought of the frightened girl who had returned to Castine. Now with all that had happened to her, she felt years older, certainly much wiser. Until they were free and the cargo ships could come, she realized she would have to use whatever means she could to keep food in the house.

As much as she detested to do so, she would go to the British to beg for food, if necessary. Their supply ships had come in, but they had not bothered to return any of the food they had taken from the people.

Her thoughts turned to John. Where was he? Was he cold? Would he remember it was nearly Christmas? Fighting the yearning to see him, she whispered a prayer: "Dear God, please watch over him. You are the only way I can reach out to him. Help him know I am praying for him. Whatever he is going through, give him the strength to bear it. It's enough to know he is alive right now, Father, but someday bring him back to me. And God, tell him I am thinking about him."

A sense of peace calmed her troubled heart and set it singing. She recalled one of the verses she had read earlier in the day to Calinta, Shonto, and Martha for their lesson.

"Where is God my maker, who giveth songs in the night?" (Job 35:10).

"I know where You are, Father. Please help me bear the burdens from day to day. The load is heavy, but it is good to know You will be there to help me carry it. Thank You for my nightsong, God," she whispered.

ROSA WRAPPED THE LAST of the three presents and laid them aside. For Shonto she had surrendered one of her favorite books, *Gulliver's Travels*. Caressing its cover, she recalled the day her mother had brought it home to her on a return trip from her native land. The legacy Elizabeth Jarden had left her daughter was a love of good books and a desire for knowledge, a legacy Rosa was pleased to pass on to Shonto, who was eager to learn. For Martha she had found a warm pair of gloves and a scarf—quite a practical gift, but of fine quality. Calinta had been the most difficult, but she finally settled on a warm shawl her mother had bought in England—one she had not lived long enough to wear.

Now for the decorations. It would be too dangerous to go into the forest for a tree. Perhaps Shonto could cut some boughs from the trees near the house. Father would understand. It would be a rather bleak Christmas as far as food was concerned. But there would be plenty of love, she vowed, as she went to join Martha and Calinta in the kitchen.

"Cally, where's Shonto?"

"Shonto in bawn," came the reply.

Rosa went in search and found him chasing a rabbit around in the hay. He caught it, holding it up by the hind legs for her to see, panting hard after his exertion.

"Supper, Missy. That's good?" he said, his round eyes shining.

"Oh, yes, Shonto. It's good. The Lord has provided once again."

"No Lord—Missy see?" He pointed to large boot tracks in the soft earth outside.

The tracks were made by the same person who had brought Martha to them. Who was he?

"Did you see the man, Shonto?"

"No, Missy. Shonto no see."

"Well, never mind for now. Whoever it is, may the Lord bless him for his goodness to us. When you have finished dressing the rabbit, would you cut some evergreen boughs for me to use as decoration? Don't go far. Just cut here close to the house."

She went on into the stall to see Nightstar, who had heard her voice and was whinnying. The mare had always been a source of joy to her, but today her thoughts were preoccupied with the mysterious footsteps. They had to be made by someone who knew their plight and was sympathetic. But who? Lieutenant Pennington? No. He would have brought the rabbit to the kitchen door. He would not see the necessity to hide his actions.

Lieutenant Pennington! He must not see the tracks. It would not be beyond him to be snooping around. Rosa went to find Shonto again.

"Shonto, when you're out getting tree limbs, would you do away with those tracks? Lieutenant Pennington mustn't see them. Whoever our benefactor is, we must protect him. He may not know we are under surveillance."

"Shonto w' do, Missy," agreed the boy.

Rosa put Martha to work cutting some red ribbon she had found, while she searched for brightly colored things to adorn the greenery. When she returned, Martha was staring off into space, the scissors still hanging in her fingers.

"What are you thinking about, Martha?" queried Rosa, studying the girl's face.

Martha did not answer but slowly began to cut the ribbons again.

"Was it John?"

A tear rolled down Martha's cheek and dropped into her lap. She nodded her head.

"John will come back to us, Martha—I feel it in my heart," promised Rosa. "God will bring him back to us."

"You love him?" asked Martha, with the direct frankness of a child.

"I love your brother very much."

Silence fell between them as Martha gave her attention to her work. Rosa watched her covertly while working at clearing the mantle over the fireplace. Would Martha know the man who had brought her to their door? Dare she ask without opening old wounds?

Martha looked up at her as if reading her thoughts, giving Rosa one of her rare smiles.

"Christmas is one of my favorite seasons, Martha," Rosa responded warmly. "This year it will be special because you are with us."

Martha appeared to be pleased at Rosa's enthusiastic response. Her face brightened, and Rosa felt compelled to ask her the question that had been on her mind. She went over and sat beside Martha, putting her arms around her thin shoulders, giving her a hug.

"Martha, you have been here with us for several weeks, and I have not asked you about what has happened to you. But I sense something is troubling you. Would it help to talk about it? Whatever you tell me will not change my love for you."

Martha dropped her head and began to cry. Rosa let her cry, knowing it was good for the tears to come. When the sobs ceased, the girl began in a monotone voice to tell a story that chilled Rosa's blood. When the massacre was over and the house had been burned, she told of being led away by two Indians. She had looked back to see where John was and saw a big Indian beating him as he was led away in another direction. She had been pushed and shoved along in the falling snow by her captors, who finally sought shelter at dusk, building a fire. They had paid no attention to her as she huddled, wretched and miserable in the cold. Feigning sleep, she had waited until they had fallen asleep and the fire was low; then she escaped into the forest. She began weeping again, wringing her hands in her lap.

"You were brought here by someone—do you know who it was?" asked Rosa, prodding her on gently.

Martha nodded. "I wandered around until I found the river and followed it toward Castine. I saw several houses, but they had all been burned. I was afraid to go near them. Then I came to the Worley house. They knew my folks. I was about to go see if anyone was around when some soldiers came by. I hid in some bushes. I overheard them say Mr. Worley wasn't among the dead and had to be hiding out nearby. They were there, looking around for what seemed a long time; then they mounted up and rode out." She paused a moment before going on.

"Their house wasn't burned as bad as ours, so I went in to see if I could find something to eat. There was a loaf of bread in the warmer of the fireplace. I ate it, sitting in a corner out of the wind. I must have fallen asleep, for I was awakened by a sound, and there was a man standing over me. He looked so ferocious, glaring down at me, that I started to scream, but he clamped a hand over my mouth.

"'No, no! You mustn't!—someone might hear!' he warned me. 'Shh! I'm not going to hurt you.'

"I must've fainted, 'cause when I woke up I was being carried into some rocks, where he laid me down. I recognized him then. It was Mr. Worley. I got awful sick, and he brought me here to you."

"But how did he escape?"

"He said he wasn't at home when the Indians came; everybody was . . . was gone when he returned," faltered Martha.

"Martha, dear, these are terrible times. We have both been through a lot. You more than me, but we shall make it together, with God's help. We must both pray for John's safe return and be strong.

"Where does this Mr. Worley stay?" Rosa added.

"Out in the rocks along the trail by the bluff," was the reply.

"In a grove of trees?" asked Rosa sharply.

"Yes, it's not far from where our farm is—do you know the place?" asked Martha, turning puzzled blue eyes at a worried Rosa.

"Yes, John and I met there. The British know about it too. They've been watching my house and that place in the rocks. They think my father may hide out there. That is not a safe place for your friend. Somehow, we must warn him of the danger." A frown wrinkled Rosa's brow.

"I know how to get in touch with him," stated Martha.

Rosa's eyes widened with surprise. Certainly she had much to learn about this brave girl. Tom Giles had been a man of great strength and religious faith. Most certainly his courage had been exemplified before his children. She had seen it in John's character.

"Tell me. He must be warned."

"He told me to hang a white cloth on the barn door if I needed him, and he would come when he could."

"Good. I will see to it right away. Ah—here's Shonto with the green boughs."

Shonto placed his armload of greenery onto the floor and returned to the barn to get the rest of his gatherings. When he came back, he had a small balsam tree, which he held proudly for Rosa to see.

"Oh, Shonto, how pretty!—where did you find it?" squealed Rosa with delight. "It's perfect!"

With Shonto's help, they managed to get it set in the corner, decorating it with bows of red ribbon and trinkets Rosa had found around the house. Her heart was full as they stood back to admire their handiwork. Calinta came in from the kitchen to see it.

"Good! Good!" she exclaimed, clapping her hands together.

A knock at the door interrupted their fun and sent them into action. Rosa hustled Martha into her room and closed the door. Shonto lingered nearby as Calinta went to answer the knock.

"Good day, Calinta," greeted Lieutenant Pennington. "I would like to speak to Miss Jarden for a moment, please."

Rosa gasped as she listened through the crack of her door. Whatever did he want? She heard Calinta invite him to wait in the kitchen and then come toward her room. Stepping back from the door, Rosa waited for Cally's call.

"Missy Rosa, dey's 'at lootenent here t' see yo'."

"Tell him to have a seat—I'll be there in a moment," instructed Rosa.

While Calinta went back with her message, Rosa turned to Martha, who was cowering in the darkened corner.

"Martha, look in the bottom of the chifforobe for a white cloth, and we'll have Shonto place it on the barn door after the lieutenant is gone," Rosa whispered. "Don't leave this room for any reason. He must not see you."

Rosa smoothed her hair and went out. Calinta hovered near the door.

"Good day, Lieutenant. Did you wish to see me?" she asked, coming toward him.

He stood to his feet as she entered the room, his dark eyes lighting up at the sight of her, and he smiled.

"Good day, Miss Jarden. You are looking quite . . . quite well."

"I'm sure you didn't come here to check my well-being, Lieutenant," Rosa replied, somewhat stiffly.

"No, although I am interested in everything about you," he answered in a mocking tone. "There is an officers' dance tomorrow night. I came to ask you to accompany me."

"Can you think of any reason I should do so?" answered Rosa, with a slight smile.

"Well, number one, you are a beautiful woman, and any man would be proud to have you on his arm; second, it would be in your best interest to do so."

His veiled threat was not lost on her. Well, two could play his game.

"Of course, Lieutenant Pennington. What time shall I be ready?" she asked coldly, striving to control the loathing she felt for the man.

"I'll pick you up at dusk." He strode to the door. "Oh, by the way—I brought you a basket of food. I thought it might come in handy about now."

As the door closed behind him, Rosa looked for something to throw at it. But since nothing was immediately available, she only stomped her foot.

"Oh, the nerve of that man!" she fumed. "He thinks he can control me with threats and food! Cally, I'm going to make him sorry he ever saw me."

"Yo' Cap'n's gurl—'at lootenent got trebble," Cally predicted with a wide-toothed grin.

Picking up the basket, Calinta searched through its contents, giving a grunt of satisfaction at finding a package of tea, along with some flour, meal, and a piece of venison.

"Wh' fo' he think he givin' us anythin'?" she mumbled, placing it on the table. "He's jus' givin' bac' wh' he dun' took."

Rosa's ire did not decrease as she went about her tasks the rest of the day. Her mind was busy planning how she would start the demise of the scheming Howland Pennington. It was well after dark when Shonto came to tell her there was a man in the barn who wished to see Martha. Rosa followed the two of them out. The lantern cast a yellow ring of light, trying to penetrate the cold, empty darkness surrounding them.

"Missy, he wa' here. Ah heered 'im!" averred Shonto, peering wide-eyed into the gloom.

"I'm here," a quiet voice spoke from the shadows. "Douse the light and stay where you are."

Shonto blew out the flame, and the three of them waited with bated breath. There was a slithering sound, followed by soft steps. They sensed rather than saw his presence when he drew near.

"What is it you wanted, girl?" asked Worley, breathing heavily.

"Miss Jarden made me put the white cloth there," answered Martha. "She wanted to speak to you."

There was dead silence before he spoke again. When he did, his voice held a note of suspicion.

"I'm listening," he responded.

"I wanted to thank you for your kindness and warn you of imminent danger. Martha told me you are hiding in a group of rocks out along the bluff trail. I know the place well. Unfortunately, the British know of the place also and will be watching. Lieutenant Pennington followed me there one day, thinking I was meeting my father, Captain Jarden. They are wanting to arrest him for aiding the Continental Army. If you continue to stay there, sooner or later, you will be discovered. I felt it my duty to warn you."

There was silence again, broken only by his heavy breathing, as he considered what she had said. Should he trust her after all he had heard about her father's ties to England?

"Girl, why are you doing this?"

"One must do what they can to fight the enemy who occupies our land, murdering and stealing from us," replied Rosa with spirit. "As a woman, I am fighting in the only way I know how."

She told him the story of all that had happened since their return from England. "The British have been lenient only because I am a woman and they hope to recapture my father. They believe I know where he is."

"And *do* you?"

"Only that he is on the high seas somewhere, fighting for freedom in his own way."

The man stood there for a moment as if deciding what to do. It suddenly occurred to Rosa that he would be hungry. There would be food left from supper.

"Would you like something to eat?" she offered.

"I wouldn't want to be no trouble to you, but it *has* been a couple of days."

It dawned on Rosa that he had brought the rabbit to them, while denying himself food. She had no idea where the thought came from, but it incited her to action.

"Shonto, tell Cally to prepare a plate of food for our guest and draw the curtains." As the lad hurried away, Rosa turned to Mr. Worley. "Sir, you are welcome to stay in the loft of our barn. I will give you some blankets to spread on the hay; you'll be warm and secure there. No one will suspect. It will be comforting to us all to have you near. Just bear in mind we are being watched. Shonto has been erasing your tracks."

"I don't want to bring calamity down upon you folks."

"Nonsense!" pressed Rosa. "We must stick together. Father would be pleased to know you are here."

"Then I'll accept your generous offer," replied Worley, without further hesitation.

"Come—we'll go in where it's warm," said Rosa, leading the way toward the light coming from the kitchen. "While you are eating I'll get you some bedding."

In the dim light of the one lamp they could afford, Rosa got a look at the man's features. He appeared to be in his early 50s with a medium-range build. His angular, friendly face was haggard, and his frank, gray eyes were haunted, almost glaring. Like all of them, he was struggling to keep above the pit of despair, having suffered the loss of his home, family, and friends.

Calinta set a plate heaped with hot food in front of him, and he ate like a man who hadn't seen food for a long time. Rosa brought blankets and a pillow. Pushing his plate aside, Worley relished the cup of hot tea Calinta brought to him.

"Lieutenant Pennington was here to invite me to the dance tomorrow evening," Rosa informed him, taking a seat across the table. "He is a despicable man, and I don't wish to go, but I was coerced into it by threats. You may rest assured I'll use the opportunity to gain what information I can."

She lowered her voice. "In Father's letter, he alluded to something big happening soon to free us from this tyranny."

"We can only hope God above will avenge the deaths of our loved ones," Worley muttered, somberly studying the tea leaves in the bottom of his cup. He reached out his hand and stroked Martha's head. She rewarded him with a smile. "It's good to see you looking well again, little one."

Rosa stood to her feet. "It is late. We must not arouse suspicion by staying up late. Shonto will show you the way to the loft. Rest well. Come, Martha."

The bed next to hers was empty when she opened her eyes the next morning. Voices were coming from the kitchen, and the smell of breakfast was in the air. Rosa turned over and lay there, thinking. Today she must make careful preparation for the dance tonight. Mentally, she went through the dresses in her closet, dismissing each one as she pictured them in her mind. She needed something more daring, more mature—like the gown her mother had worn to the ball in London. Her breath caught in her throat. She was about the size of her mother now. Why not? Later she would try it on and see if Calinta needed to take it in.

With that settled in her thinking, Rosa threw back the covers, donned her robe and slippers, and headed into the warmth of the kitchen.

"Oh, am I the last one to arrive for breakfast?" she greeted the group in mock surprise.

"That you are, lass," responded Mr. Worley, almost cheerfully.

"Yo' sleep like yo' was dead, Missy Rosa," Cally laughed, placing a meager plate of food before her.

"It's Martha's fault," Rosa bantered goodnaturedly. "She deserted me. Besides, it was probably because the sky was so dark." Rosa peeked out between the curtains. "Looks like we're in for some more snow," she added, taking her place at the table. Calinta came to fill her cup.

The mood was light for the first time in many days as they

talked in subdued voices. Each understood the common, underlying grief and suffering of the others, constituting a silent pact that knitted them together.

Lingering over a last cup of tea, Rosa saw Shonto lift his head as if listening to something outside. He raised a warning hand, causing those around the table to fall silent. Slipping into the stable, he returned in a moment, laying a finger over his lips.

"Redcoats! Dey's lookin' at tracks," he whispered excitedly.

"Quick, Cally—take the dishes away," Rosa exclaimed, her mind racing. "Martha, Mr. Worley, come with me to my room! I'll hide you there."

"Hurry!" she insisted as Worley hesitated. "They may demand to search the house." She shoved the reluctant man in that direction.

Barely had they made their hasty retreat when there was the sound of hard boots on the porch. Shouts could be heard outside. A loud pounding on the door was enough to strike fear in any heart. Rosa heard Cally's quick steps to answer the door and went out yawning, still dressed in her robe, as soldiers rudely pushed the black woman aside to enter.

"What is the meaning of this?" demanded Rosa, angrily.

The one to answer was the corporal who had tried to bar her from entering her house earlier. His eyes were cold and his manner bore no warmth as he answered.

"We've orders to search the premises."

"And who is responsible for this . . . this . . . outrage?"

"I am," replied a familiar voice. Lieutenant Pennington stepped through the group at the door.

Rosa felt her face pale a little at the sight of him, unaware of the desirable sight she made standing there, slender form wrapped in a blue robe and golden hair cascading around her shoulders.

"Do what you must," she said, haughtily. "But please allow me the privacy of my own room."

"As you wish, Miss Jarden," he agreed, mockingly, with a slight bow.

Rosa returned to her room and locked the door, relieved to be away from the admiring glances of ogling soldiers. Martha and Worley were nowhere to be seen. They had hidden themselves.

"Are they gone?" Martha asked from under the bed.

"Shhh! No," Rosa answered in a whisper. "Stay where you are."

She sat down before the mirror to brush her hair. Footsteps could be heard overhead as they searched her father's room. After what seemed like an eternity, she heard a call for Lieutenant Pennington come from the direction of the stable. It was then she remembered the blankets she had given Worley. Waiting with bated breath for the inevitable, she jumped at his knock, even though she was expecting it.

"Just a minute, please," she called out, removing her robe to throw it around her again as if in haste. "Don't move," she warned in a whisper to those in hiding. Opening the door, she swung it wide to indicate she had nothing to hide, knowing his eyes would take the room in at a glance. She was not disappointed. When his penetrating gaze returned to rest on her, she blushed, feeling ill at ease with him invading her privacy.

"Come to the kitchen, please." His voice was controlled, void of emotion. "There are some questions to be asked."

Rosa followed him meekly, careful to close the door behind her. When she entered, she was not surprised to see a young soldier holding the bedding from the hayloft. He appeared embarrassed in her presence.

"One of my men found this in the loft. I presume you have an explanation for it being there?"

"Oh, that," Rosa sighed, as if with relief. "Shonto found some tracks outside the stable one day, and he has been keeping a close watch on Nightstar. After all, she was stolen once, and we didn't wish for it to happen again." She saw him stiffen and knew her remark had hit home.

"Can you explain this?" he asked, brusquely, pointing to the piece of white cloth the corporal held out.

"Looks like a piece of material I tore up to put salve on Nightstar's wounds when your men brought her back," she responded, looking up at him with wide-eyed innocence. "Where did you find it?"

"It was on the ground outside one of the stable doors."

"Probably stuck to Shonto's foot as he went out that way," Rosa replied, unperturbed. "Now if you will excuse me, Lieutenant, I have a lot to do before accompanying you to the dance tonight."

She derived great satisfaction at his discomfort, as the eyes of the other troops turned on him in surprise. One soldier elbowed the other but beat a hasty retreat after receiving a dark look of rebuke.

The soldiers withdrew and Rosa turned away, hoping her trembling would go unnoticed. She did not see the calculated look Pennington gave her before following his men. She motioned to Shonto to her side. "Let me know when you're sure they're all gone."

Returning to her room, she found Worley and Martha waiting for her, standing just inside the door. The girl's face was white with unspent emotion.

"You are safe," she informed them. "They're leaving."

"I've gotta hand it to you, lass—you're sure a cool one," Mr. Worley declared with admiration. "Kinda a chip off the old block of your daddy."

"Dey's all gon', Missy Rosa," Shonto informed her from the door. "I'll hep Mista Worley put his bed back."

Worley patted Martha on the head and followed Shonto out. Calinta came in to flutter around Rosa and Martha. It was plain to see the whole episode had upset her greatly.

"Um mmp. Yo' sure is de Cap'n's girl. Cap'n wo' be . . . wo' be . . ."

"Proud of me?" Rosa laughed, without humor, finishing the sentence for her. "You're right, Cally. That he would be. But right now I feel like I want to cry."

Calinta put her arms around the shaking girl. "Yo' jes go to cry, Babee. Yo' did good!"

Gradually becoming calm again, Rosa noted Cally's use of the new Christmas word, baby, she had taught her to spell. She suspected her pupil was retaining more than she would readily admit.

The rest of the morning was spent getting together things she would need for the dance that evening. Much to her surprise, no alterations to her mother's gown of white taffeta with lace inserts were needed. It fit as if it had been made for her. However, the low-cut neckline made her blush as she thought of the bold eyes that would be watching her at the dance.

Martha clapped with delight as Rosa chose a pearl necklace to finish out her costume. Her father had brought it home from the south seas for her beloved mother.

"This will do, Cally, but I will need a lacy handkerchief and some matching gloves. And, oh dear! What will I wear for slippers? I'm not sure Mother's satin ones will fit me. Bring them back with you too."

When all was in readiness, they went to the kitchen to have a hot cup of tea. Shonto and Mr. Worley came in from the barn and sat near the fire, warming their hands.

"Mr. Worley, tell me what you know about the war to the south," Rosa asked. "It's hard for us to know anything with all the fighting going on so far away. My father told me the British have been a menace to the ships carrying cargo into the ports. Why are we fighting to be free from British rule?"

"Well, lass," he began, clearing his throat. "The patriots of this country are getting tired of being taxed to death by an unrelenting government so far away. They come and rob us of all our possessions without offering to pay us. We don't even own the ground we work so hard to clear for raising crops. If we don't abide by the British decrees, they turn the Indians on us to murder and plunder.

"The war, for the most part, is being fought down below Boston. I heard it was going better with General Washington's forces since the French are helping and that they were going to send help up this way. Well, sir, when they did, they just stayed offshore, waiting for reinforcements and got caught by the arrival of the British ships coming in with more guns and troops.

"I heard the shooting and saw the fires that day, so I grabbed my gun 'n' left my family to go 'n' see what was coming off. General Lovell and Captain Saltonstall scuttled their ships up on the Penobscot and were fleeing into the forests. Seems they couldn't get together on a battle plan after they landed Paul Revere and his men on the heights overlooking Castine. They could have taken Castine, but they stalled, giving Mowatt and his men time to complete Fort George.

"That's about all I knew, lass, 'cepting they ain't never going to win this war until they clean out this nest of thievin', murderin' Tories. And that's what I told Paul Revere when I last saw him there in the forest. I hope he made it back with my message. When I returned home . . . well, you know the rest." His voice broke, and he lowered his head.

8

ROSA SURVEYED HERSELF in the mirror, satisfied with the lovely image she saw there. She had piled her golden hair high on her head, allowing some of the curls to hang tantalizingly free around her face.

"You look like a fairy princess!" Martha exclaimed. "But you need a magic wand."

Rosa turned to take Martha's face between her hands. "If I had a magic wand, Martha, I would put everything back as it should be," she said softly. "But then, I wouldn't have you here to live with me, would I?"

"Shhh," Rosa cautioned as a knock sounded at the door. "That will be Lieutenant Pennington. Don't make a sound until we are gone. Say a prayer for me, won't you? What I am doing tonight is very important. I will tell you all about it tomorrow. Good night."

Rosa accepted the white fur cape Calinta held for her, then walked to the parlor where Howland Pennington was waiting. He was standing with a hand on the mantle, looking somberly into the fire, presenting a striking appearance in his dress uniform with its polished saber hanging at his side. He would have captured the heart of any woman—even hers, had it not been for the disdain she felt for him.

At her soft step, he looked up, transfixed. "Ah, you are

more beautiful than I imagined." He took her hands, drawing her into the light. His eyes blazed into hers, and she could see his lips tighten. There was the slight odor of rum on his breath. She was glad Cally came into the room. Freeing her hands, she adjusted her wrap.

"Come, Lieutenant—we would not want to be late for the party, would we?" Rosa said saucily, while quaking inside at being alone with him.

Concern was written on Calinta's face, and her hand crept to her throat in search of her fetish, which was missing. That fact curiously impressed Rosa as she gave her one last glance.

"Good night, Cally. Don't wait up. I'm certain the lieutenant will make sure nothing happens to me. Isn't that right, sir?"

He declined to answer, taking her arm to escort her to the waiting carriage. Rosa recognized it as the one owned by the tavern keeper. It was probably confiscated like everything else.

She had overheard her father and Caleb talking about the "shaving mills," a name given to small boats of all types used by the British to go up and down the coastline, helping themselves to whatever goods they could find without restitution of any kind. No concern was given for people who had worked so hard to raise the crops or produce the goods. They seemed to enjoy treating them like slaves of England to be trampled underfoot by the occupying army.

"You are very quiet, Miss Jarden. Would you like to tell me what you are thinking?"

"I'm afraid you would not find it amusing, Lieutenant," she said guardedly.

The ride was short, stopping before Catuna House, where there was a large hall upstairs. The entrance had been decorated with fragrant garlands of balsam and pine. Inside, the same festive mood had been set, and a roaring fire warmed the room. Violinists warmed up their instruments and began to play. Couples began to move out onto the floor to dance a minuet.

"Shall we join them?" Lieutenant Pennington asked, taking her cape.

While she waited, Rosa looked around the room. There were fewer women than men, since many had not brought their wives with them. Those who were there gazed at her with interest and envy. One of them was the innkeeper's daughter, who whispered something to a woman nearby and giggled. Rosa turned her attention away. Across the room, standing in a group of men, she spotted Captain Mowatt. He had not seen her, but some of the men he was talking to did and lost interest in what he was saying. He turned to see what had attracted their attention and seemed taken aback to see her there.

Rosa smiled and nodded her head in recognition. He cleared his throat noisily, returning to his conversation. But Rosa vowed that before the evening was over he would dance with her.

Her escort returned to claim her, and they moved out onto the floor with the others. Lieutenant Pennington was an excellent dancer and led her boldly through the steps. Rosa found herself enjoying the occasion in spite of the reservations she had in coming. She smiled at everyone, much to Howland Pennington's discomfort.

"Must you do that?" he scowled.

"What, Lieutenant?" asked Rosa, with feigned innocence.

"Smile and flirt with these men!" he answered between clenched teeth, keeping an outward smile on his face. "You've got them all moon-eyed over you."

"Why, Lieutenant, I think you are jealous. I hardly see why you should be, since we scarcely know each other."

Rosa felt his hand tighten on hers until it hurt. It frightened her. Perhaps she had gone too far. She must be careful. It was a very tight line she was walking. She smiled up at him.

When the dance ended, as chance would have it they were near Captain Mowatt and his colleagues. Rosa fanned herself daintily.

"May I get you something to drink?" the lieutenant asked.

"Please, Lieutenant, and I assure you I will be in good company while you are gone," she said demurely, smiling at Captain Mowatt, who had turned her way.

"Good evening, Captain. Why are you not dancing? Is it because you have no partner?"

"My partner, Miss Jarden, is in England."

"Oh, I'm sorry to hear that, Captain. I would be delighted to dance with you. Perhaps we can persuade Lieutenant Pennington . . ."

"Persuade me to do what?" He spoke up at her elbow, handing her a cup of punch.

"Why, to let Captain Mowatt have the next dance," Rosa replied, with a bright smile, knowing he could hardly refuse.

"Of course," the lieutenant conceded, but his smooth answer belied the seething current underneath.

Sipping her drink, Rosa could tell he was angry. Little did he know she was not done with him yet. She handed him the cup as the music began.

This dance was a waltz that kept the partners closer together, making it possible for conversation. In spite of his weight, the captain was light on his feet. Even though he maintained a stern expression, she felt comfortable in his presence.

"This partner you spoke of. She is your wife?"

"Yes, Miss Jarden."

"You must miss her very much."

"That is true," he answered wistfully, softening a little. "I will be glad when I return to England."

"Will that be soon, Captain Mowatt?"

"Perhaps, but . . . ahem . . . that is nothing I should discuss with you, Miss Jarden," was his gruff answer. "Tell me—why are you here tonight?"

"Don't you know?" she asked, glad he had given her the opening she was hoping for. "Lieutenant Pennington threatened me into coming. He said it would be in my best interest to do so. I've come to believe the lieutenant is a cruel, ambitious man who schemes to get what he wants. I do not wish to be here, Captain, and I'm afraid to have him take me home."

She looked up at him with candid, brown eyes. "Why, if you're not careful, sir, he'll be taking your command away. Did you know he brought soldiers in to search our home this morning on some trumped-up charge, and I was just out of my bed? I . . . I was so humiliated. Those soldiers were all ogling at me so . . . so wantonly.

"Surely, Captain," Rosa went on, her heart beating fast, "that is not your way. You are a husband, a father. Would you want your daughter treated in such a manner?"

He did not answer, but gave a studied, calculating look in the direction of Lieutenant Pennington, who was dancing with the daughter of the tavern owner. Feeling she had hit a soft spot, Rosa went on.

"When my father left, he told me I had nothing to fear from you, that I would be treated well."

"Where *is* your father, Miss Jarden?"

"A sea captain brought me a letter some time back," Rosa replied candidly. "After my father left here, he was boarded and captured by pirates, but he later escaped. Now he's somewhere on the high seas with a newly commissioned ship."

When he made no further comment, she ventured to ask, "Captain, would you see me safely home, please?"

He did not answer, and Rosa thought he had not heard.

"Captain, would you take me home? If not for Father's sake, please—for mine."

"How old are you, lass?"

"I am 16, going on 17."

"Just the age of my Susan," he muttered to himself.

He looked down at her as they dipped and swayed to the music. The way she wore her hair made her look older than her 16 years. Curved lips smiled up at him, revealing a row of even white teeth. Entreating brown eyes looked back at him unafraid. A great sense of longing for his wife and daughter came over him. Tearing his eyes away, he mumbled, "I'll be glad when this God-forsaken war is over."

"I beg your pardon, Captain?"

"Harumph!" he cleared his throat and appeared a little embarrassed. "I was saying, I will escort you home, Miss Jarden. But now that my men have had a look at you, I would advise you to stay close to home."

When the music stopped, he led her over to where Lieutenant Pennington was standing with several others.

"Lieutenant, Miss Jarden is feeling ill. I am going to take her home. You men stay and enjoy yourselves." He turned to give an order to a soldier standing nearby.

"Corporal, bring Miss Jarden her coat, and get a carriage to the door."

Rosa stood with her head down, not daring to look at Howland Pennington. She could feel his dark gaze upon her. Relief came when the corporal came to inform them the carriage was waiting. Not a word was spoken on the short ride up the hill to the Jarden house. Snow had begun to fall, blown like dust across the road by a stiff wind. When the carriage came to a halt before the gate, Captain Mowatt helped her to the door.

"Miss Jarden, you are a beautiful and lovely girl." His blue eyes were sober as he gazed down at her. "Your father must be very proud of you. I will see to it you are not threatened again." He spoke brusquely, bowing slightly.

"Thank you, Captain. And Captain?" Rosa laid her hand on his arm as he was turning away. With a rush of emotion, she continued softly, "Your wife must be a wonderful woman. I pray God will give you a safe return to your family. Good-bye."

Calinta had the door unlocked, and Rosa let herself in to find they had been watching through the darkened window.

"Chile, yo' back so soon!" she exclaimed happily.

"Yes, Cally. I asked Captain Mowatt to bring me home." She giggled. "I wouldn't want to be in Lieutenant Pennington's shoes tomorrow. Now, help me get into something more comfortable, and I'll tell you all about it over a cup of hot tea."

They gathered around the table and listened intently as she told them all that had happened. Shonto clapped his hands in glee, but Cally appeared more reserved.

"Missy, yo' make bad frien' . . . he be back."

"I'm afraid she's right, lass," Mr. Worley agreed. "You have made a mortal enemy. Unless he is sent away, you will hear from him again. He is not the kind of man who will give up easily. I know men, and this one is not to be trusted."

Rosa knew they were right, but she refused to allow their alarm to daunt her spirit. She would face each day as it came.

"Tonight is Christmas Eve!" she announced gaily, changing the subject. "Let's go in by the fire, and I'll read you the Christmas story."

When she had finished reading, Martha sat in rapt silence. Shonto's eyes glowed with a soft light. There were tears in Mr. Worley's eyes, and Cally sat thoughtfully looking into the fire.

"I have a gift for each of you," she said, laying the book aside.

Later, long after the house had grown quiet and Martha's breathing had grown regular with sleep, Rosa lay awake, reflecting on the hectic day that had ended so peacefully. Their troubles had been pushed to the background for a short while as they opened the gifts and enjoyed some sweet cakes Cally had made.

Her thoughts went to John. Would he remember it was Christmas? Would he be thinking of her? Oh, John, I miss you so! Please, dear God—don't let me lose faith. Give me my nightsong that I may be strong.

The next morning, Mr. Worley did not appear for breakfast. Calinta indicated he may be sleeping late, but Shonto came in to inform them he was gone.

"Gone?—what do you mean gone?" Rosa exclaimed.

"He no sleep in bed. Gone."

"I know where he went," offered Martha, with a solemn face. "He went back to his home. He's thinkin' about . . . them."

"Of course! Poor man. He must miss his loved ones so." He had gone when he knew the snow would cover his tracks. They could only pray for his safe return.

Nearly a month went by, and Rosa was beginning to think something had happened to Mr. Worley when he surprised them by showing up well after dark one evening. Haggard, hollow-eyed, cold, and hungry, his clothes in tatters, he hovered over the fire, strangely different. His already-worn boots were beyond repair. She could see his toes showing through the tops, giving evidence he had traveled a great distance while he was gone. He gratefully accepted the hot food Calinta warmed up for him, sitting near the stove while he ate. Curiously his eyes kept going to Martha, who sat at the table working on a lesson Rosa had assigned her.

Questions were crowding Rosa's mind, but she withheld any attempt to press him for answers, waiting politely until he had appeased his hunger.

Martha finished her lesson and closed her book. With a sigh, she asked, "Rosa, may I be excused?"

"Yes, Martha. It's getting on toward your bedtime. I'll be along shortly."

Worley mopped up the last of the broth with his bread, stuffed it into his mouth, and handed the empty bowl to Cally. His eyes followed Martha from the room, then taking up his cup of tea, he came to the table where Rosa sat.

"Well, sir, fust off, I want to apologize for leaving so sudden like. I hope it didn't bring yuh any more worry than yuh already have on yer head, lass. I just had to go back—although I found it wasn't a good idea. Met up with a band of Indians not far from here and would've lost my scalp but for the fact they caught a young boy hiding out in the bushes. I circled around and watched from a distance as they took him to the top of the hill, tortured him, then burned him at a stake." He lowered his voice. "It was that young George Giles who'd escaped. He must've come back to his home."

"How terrible!" Rosa gasped, feeling sick in the pit of her stomach. "Poor George!"

"Well, sir, when I saw there wasn't nothing I could do against so many, I made off to leave. It was then I saw the soldier astride his horse back in the trees. I recognized him. It was that Pennington fella. He's been behind this whole murderous plan. The man is more bloodthirsty than those poor savages he likkers up.

"Well, sir, I knew I didn't dare move. He'd have seen me for sure. So I had to take my chances and stay put. The whole thing was hideous. Even Pennington couldn't stomach it for long, and when he rode out I turned and ran, heading straight for the Penobscot River.

"There's a boat hidden along the shore where some of us used to cross over. I rowed up river to make contact with a friend for a horse, but his outfit had been burned, his family destroyed. I headed out on foot to Bucksport. There's a patriot living there, and I knew he would know how the war was going on.

"When I arrived, I found things had been going pretty hard for folks around there too. But he made me welcome, and we talked a lot. He told me General Washington had turned the war around and that the British were being routed. He said it would only be a matter of time until the war would be over." He leaned back in his chair and wearily brushed his hand across his eyes.

"A strange thing happened on my way back. I was beaching the boat in our hiding place when I spotted several canoes heading upriver. I was pretty well hidden, and they didn't see me, but I got a good look at them.

"There was a fellow in the center of one of the boats that didn't look like an Indian. He was dressed like one, but his face was white. I was so shocked at what I saw, I forgot where I was and stood up for a better look. Well, sir, this fella turned his head and looked straight at me. I saw a look of recognition and surprise in his face and thought it would be all over with me, but he turned his head back without a sound, and they went on. It was John Giles!"

Rosa's heart gave a leap in her breast. "Are . . . are you sure?" she managed to stammer.

Worley gave her a strange look. "Sure? I'd know that face anywhere," he affirmed, nodding his head. "I watched that young'un grow up. Yes, sir, it was John Giles, all right." He got to his feet.

"Do you have a gun here in the house?"

"Why do you ask?"

"I just think it would be best to have one for protection in case some of these people get desperate."

"Cally, do you know if Father had a gun?"

"Cap'n gun in his room," Cally answered, drying her wet hands on her apron. She took a lamp and led the way upstairs. She pointed to the closet that held the Captain's clothes.

Rosa looked for the weapon but found none. The British soldiers must have found it and taken it when they searched the house. Rosa wondered what else they had helped themselves to.

Cally went to the bed and reached under the pillow to pull out a pistol. Carefully, she handed the gun to Worley, who examined it, grunting his satisfaction.

"Not as good as a rifle, but it'll do," he responded, sticking it into his belt.

"Mr. Worley, here is one of Father's coats. It may be a little large for you, but it will be warm. I don't know about these boots." Rosa held them up for him to see. "If you think they fit you well enough, you may have them."

"Bless you, lass. You have such a kind heart. I'm beholdin' to you."

"We must all help one another, Mr. Worley. You've brought us renewed hope." Rosa looked around the room. "Cally, did Shonto go to bed?"

"I think so, Missy," was the answer.

"Well, I think that is a good suggestion for all of us," Rosa stated, leading the way down the stairs. "Good night."

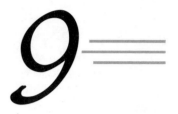

9

JOHN GILES AWOKE to a cold, gray dawn with the dread of facing still another day of beatings. He had learned long ago to endure the hard work imposed on him by the squaws, who beat him with long sticks if he so much as raised his eyes to look at them. He was not allowed to speak. To them, he was just a beast of burden to remain tied up like a dog when he was not needed. There had been days when he was forced to crawl on all fours while his back was laden with firewood to be hauled back to camp.

The boots and clothes he wore the day he was captured were taken from him, and the old Indian garb he had been given to replace them now hung in tatters. At least he still had his hair, although it had grown below his shoulders. He wore it back Indian fashion, bound with a leather thong. It was plain his captors did not wish for him to identify in any way with the white man's world, so he had set out to learn their language and ways, hoping to be treated with more respect.

The soft tread of moccasin-clad feet announced the beginning of another day of activity in the camp. John stretched his cramped body and sat up. To be caught in a prone position when they came for him meant only another beating. Sitting in the semidarkness of the crude, filthy shelter, he lent himself to meditation, which had been his habit since that fateful day. His father's last prayer still lingered, indelibly imprinted in his mind; he clung to it for hope and courage.

His thoughts went to Martha and George. Were they still alive? Did they ever think of him? The image of a golden-haired face with shining eyes floated into his consciousness. "It has always been you, John. I will wait for you." Those words alone had kept his hope alive. A great shudder went over him as he relived the last parting moments they had shared so long ago.

A sound outside his pen attracted his attention. Two large, leather-bound legs and feet came into view. It was Madowock. As the covering over the door was removed, John tried to search his mind for a reason Madowock would be coming for him and found none. He held his head high as the leather collar was removed from his neck and the bindings from his hands.

"Come," he was instructed in a guttural native tongue.

Off in the mist, John could hear a tom-tom giving off a slow, rhythmic beat. He had been in the village long enough to know this was a call for the people to gather, usually preceding an important event or someone's demise. Madowock had not brought his beating stick. This caused John to wonder.

When they arrived at the ceremonial fire, the circle of people opened an aisle to allow them through. Standing straight and tall as a willow, John looked around at the people who were staring at him, talking in whispers.

To his right stood Madowock's woman and daughter. They were actually smiling at him, a fact he could not comprehend. These were the ones who had administered the cruelty upon him.

Madowock held up his hand, and the people became silent. He began to speak, and a gasp came from many in the crowd. John could not believe what he was hearing. It seemed that Madowock's daughter, One Who Comes Running, wanted him as her husband. A young brave, the one called Wypitlock, separated himself from the crowd to step within a few feet of John.

"Is this the one who crawled around like a dog? A slave of squaws? Why would she want a dog warrior instead of a brave warrior?" He cried angrily to the people, hitting his breast. "If he wishes to become a brave, let him earn the right!"

The challenge hit a chord in the raucous crowd. They screamed and called out, "Dog Warrior! Dog Warrior!"

Madowock held up his hand for silence. When the din had quieted, he shouted, "So be it! The Dog Warrior shall earn the right to become a brave."

John was taken on hunts and taught the Indian art of tracking and crawling through the bush undetected. He made his own tomahawk and gratefully accepted the new buckskin pants, jacket, and moccasins, complete with the leather leggings One Who Comes Running made for him. No longer was he required to sleep in the filthy pen with a collar around his neck like an animal, but was included in the household of Madowock. One Who Comes Running was delighted, talking to him with her eyes, smiling shyly at his clumsiness in trying to master the art of making spearheads.

Always at home in the forest, John enjoyed his new freedom, although on their distant forays he was never out of visual contact with someone from the tribe.

One mild winter day, as was his habit, he was down by the creek practicing his skill with the tomahawk and spear. Over and over he threw the weapons, using his wrist as Madowock had shown him. Sure and true, his weapon found its mark with deadly accuracy. It appeared he was so intent in his work he did not see Madowock's approach.

"If I was the enemy, Sannup, you would be dead," Madowock greeted him, beckoning with his hand. "Come."

"If Dog Warrior had not known your tread, my friend, *you* would have been dead," John returned truthfully, falling in step beside the elder Indian.

Other warriors joined them, among whom was Wypitlock, his mortal enemy, who gave John an evil grin and boastingly said, "Soon, Dog Warrior, your bones will rot in the dust."

They started off through the forest at a run, Madowock allowing Wypitlock to set the pace. John realized he was being tested and soon proved his prowess with his adversary, jumping the logs and fallen trees like a deer. Red squirrels, taking advantage of a pause in the harsh winter weather to search for food, scurried before them. Whitetail deer lifted their heads to fearlessly watch the strange sight of the buckskin-clad figures gliding through the forest.

Stimulated by the exertion, John's every sense became keener as they raced onward like free, wild creatures of an untamed land. Among the few stops made was one to take a cold, invigorating drink of water at one of the many ponds. The hate in Wypitlock's eyes followed John's every movement.

The pace, which would test the endurance of any man, did not let up but continued far into the night, taking them farther and farther away from the village. Finally, Madowock spoke a command, stepping from the trail to seek shelter under a tree. Bracing himself against the trunk, he fell instantly asleep. The rest followed suit. To John, it seemed he had just closed his eyes when he felt Madowock's big foot shaking him. He accepted the piece of dried venison Madowock handed him, eating on the run.

By midday they had reached the upper reaches of a river. Here they uncovered three large birch canoes they had hidden in a covert. John was placed in the middle between Madowock and Wypitlock, his mortal enemy. He was glad Madowock was to his back, an action he felt was not just happenstance.

Swift, sure strokes sent the canoes flying through the water with the current. Daylight caught up with them far down the river. Whatever their mission, it seemed imperative they make haste. He could only hope he would not be required to take a life to prove his prowess as a warrior. He tried to push the thought from his mind by concentrating on the wildlife along the riverbank. Most of the birds had long taken their flight southward, but the whitetails were plentiful.

On their second day on the river, a slight movement on

the shore to his right caught John's attention. Turning his head, he looked right into the surprised face of a white man. It was the first he had seen since the Indians had taken him, but one he remembered as a friend of his father. Turning his face quickly, less he attract the attention of the others, he fished around in his memory for a name. Wearley, Worley? Yes, that was it: Worley. Had the man recognized him? Probably not. He looked more like an Indian than ever with his long, dark hair and skin browned by long hours in the sun.

Did that mean they were on the Penobscot heading for the village of Castine? Suddenly, his heart began to beat faster as he strained his eyes to catch sight of a familiar landmark. The river was broadening considerably, but the Indians soon guided the canoes in close to the shore, where they entered a small tributary in which to hide their craft. Once on ground, they struck off in an easterly direction, then turned south. Their movement was more cautious now, and they stopped often to listen. John glided from tree to tree, among red maple, birch, and pine, tomahawk in hand. Their journey ended in a dense grove of balsam trees that bore evidence of having been used many times before.

John knew without being told that searching for wood was his job. Since most of the fallen wood nearby had been used, he had to seek farther out. There in the soft forest floor he saw the hoofprints of a horse, preserved by the thick canopy of trees. They were old and probably would have been washed out if they had been made in a more exposed area.

A glance at his companions told him he was not being observed. He knelt to examine them more closely. Something vague stirred in his memory. Dismissing it from his mind with a grunt, he picked up his bundle of wood and headed back to camp. There were nine of them in all. The other eight sat in a circle talking in low voices, but his approach interrupted their quiet conversation, and they fell silent. They seemed oblivious to his actions, but he knew better. If he made a move to escape, they would be all over him. Wypitlock, especially, would not miss a chance to take out his vengeance.

No one offered to help John start a fire, but all sat cross-legged, watching him nurse a tiny finger of light until it became a blaze. Madowock grunted with satisfaction, holding his hands out to the warmth. It was plain they were waiting for someone, and soon the atmosphere became more relaxed. John joined the silent group, settling down beside Madowock. Stoic faces gave no hint of what they were thinking as they stared into the fire.

Darkness slowly invaded the forest, and a cold wind began to blow, moaning in the trees overhead. John put more wood on the fire and was about to regain his seat when Madowock put out his arm, restraining him. "Sit there," he said, indicating a rock off in the shadows.

John did as he was told. Moments later, he heard the ring of a horse's hoof on a rock and knew the long-awaited caller had arrived. Whoever it was, Madowock did not wish for him to be seen by the stranger.

Creaking leather, along with the impatient stomping of the animal, broke the stillness of the wooded area. John kept his eyes on those seated around the fire as sturdy footsteps came toward them. None gave any indication of another presence, letting him know Madowock and his companions had no fear of their visitor. That could mean they knew who it was and had met him in like manner before.

John rested his chin upon his knees, folding his arms across them so that only his eyes were visible. A tall, lithe figure carrying a large pouch strode into the circle of light, hesitated briefly, then seated himself beside Madowock. He kept the pouch in his lap. Light from the fire lit up the man's features that had been hidden by his hat. John sucked in a deep breath as he recognized the man to be Lieutenant Pennington.

As usual, nothing was said until Madowock initiated the conversation. In sharp contrast to the others, the soldier, in his flashy uniform, sat tall and defiant, glancing impatiently into the shadows around him. John was in his direct line of vision and felt the stiffening of the hairs on the back of his neck as the dark, intense gaze swept over him.

Madowock began to speak, and he was forgotten for the moment as Pennington's attention returned to the circle around the fire. When it came Pennington's time to speak, John could tell he was trying hard to hold himself in check. His voice was sharp as he complained about the botched-up job they had done before.

"I instructed you to kill them all," he said caustically, trying to conceal the anger in his voice. "But you let several of them escape. Dead men tell no tales!"

They merely stared at him with glittering eyes, silent and unwavering. John observed Madowock looking in his direction, and he knew for certain that he was one of those who had escaped death. From their demeanor, he could tell the Indians were not taking kindly to Pennington's scolding, remaining aloof until he addressed the reason he had sent for them. Little did the lieutenant realize how close to death he was. Had it not been for the promised payment, his scalp would have been lifted.

"I have another job for you," Pennington continued with rancor, unaware of his precarious position, "and I don't want anything to go wrong with this one. I want you to bring a girl to me here. Half the pay will be given to you now. Take care that she is not harmed in any way, and the rest will be given to you tomorrow night."

"Where girl?" Madowock muttered, unperturbed, his eyes on the pouch in Pennington's lap.

"There is a trail that runs along the bluff. Just off that is a grove of trees surrounding a hideaway in some rocks. A note, from a lover she pines for, will bring her there when the sun is high. She will be waiting for him in the rocks."

John's heart leaped within his breast. He knew well the covert Pennington was describing. His eyes grew dim as he remembered his last visit there.

"What girl's name?" he heard Madowock ask, knowing full well the answer before it came.

"Jarden—Rosa Jarden," Pennington answered, describing her. "Not one hair of her head is to be harmed. Do you understand? I want her, and I want her in good condition—or no pay."

"Make squaw?" Madowock asked, a knowing smile breaking the somberness of his face.

"Make squaw," replied Pennington thickly.

John sat frozen in place, staring at Pennington in disbelief at what he had just heard. The whole dastardly scheme to lure Rosa out to the wilderness was so Pennington, the man she had scorned, could get even with her. His intentions would be less than noble, driven by his desire to possess her at all costs. Something cold and nameless reared its ugly head inside of John, and he fought off the urge to send his tomahawk to its sure mark. To do so would only mean the loss of his own life. He would have to wait.

Pennington got to his feet, dropping the heavy pouch to the ground in front of Madowock, who immediately searched its contents. Holding up a bottle of rum, the leader gave a grunt of satisfaction. Turning on his heel, the lieutenant walked to his waiting mount. Soon John heard him moving off through the trees. Still he did not leave his seat until Madowock motioned for him. As a precaution, he kept his head averted from the fire. Pennington may be lurking out there yet, and it would not do for him to be recognized.

Madowock and the others were gleefully downing the bottles of rum that had been included in the pouch. It was not long before the rum took effect, and they became boastful and boisterous. Wypitlock waved a bottle under John's nose and danced around him with glee.

"Soon we will fight, Dog Warrior," he snarled, "and I will leave your blood in the dust."

"You are drunk," John answered with disgust, turning his back on him as a sign of bravery.

Wypitlock lunged, but John stepped to one side, allowing the brave to go flying headfirst into the pine needles, where he scrambled to his feet with the bottle still in his hand. Giving a blood-curdling cry, Wypitlock pulled his knife and advanced toward John. His face was distorted, and his malevolent eyes glittered.

"Soon!" he hissed, turning away.

John settled himself near the fire, feigning sleep. He would not feel safe until his companions were lulled into a drunken stupor. Wypitlock sat across from him, consuming his bottle, casting baleful glances his direction. If Madowock slumbered first, he would have to be on his guard. Not that he feared the others. They had accepted his presence as a matter of fact, ignoring him. On the other hand, Wypitlock's malice had gone far beyond a feeling of jealousy because of his love for One Who Comes Running. Now it was much deeper than that. Wypitlock would not be happy until he was dead.

To keep awake, John tried to sort out what he had heard. Recalling Pennington's sharp rebuke, he felt sure the man was referring to the attack on his family. Had not Madowock's silent glance told the story? The men had met in this very spot to lay the murderous plot. He felt the blood in his veins heat at the thought. For what price did his family die? Some gold and a few bottles of rum for the destruction of who knows how many souls. Though it had sustained him in the early days of his captivity, the memory of his father kneeling to pray for his children had slowly faded as John struggled to stay alive. The intense mental anguish accompanied by constant ridicule and abuse made keeping his sanity an effort that was continuously pushed to the edge.

Beaten into submission, he had eventually lost identity with many commonalities from his life previously. Though he could not return her love, he would always be grateful to One Who Comes Running for her intervention. Had it not been for her, he would still be a beast of burden living in the filth and stench of his own excrement. Little wonder he had taken on a savage way of existence. But now he knew he could not go on with the pretense. He would not be a part of this!

His thoughts turned to Rosa. Seeing her face in his mind's eye during those long, troubled nights had kept his spirit alive. Once these projected intruders caught sight of her, there would be no turning back. Pennington was the same as a dead man; of that he was sure. Rosa's safety lay in John's hands alone. How and what he could do he would not know until the time came. He must ever keep alert—and pray for an opportunity to escape.

Pray! When had he last uttered a prayer? Had it been in those early days when he lay bruised and bleeding, threatened with death every day, until hope of rescue or escape was gone? He was no longer his former self, having developed instincts similar to those of an animal and ready to accept any scrap of humane treatment. To adopt a new way of life seemed perfectly natural to survive, but now he must return to his God-given identity and remain his father's son, John Giles.

As far as he knew, he was the only one left. Therefore, it was his responsibility to fulfill his father's dying wish. Overhead, the forlorn sound of the wind through the boughs of the trees seemed to echo the silent cry of his heart as he reached heavenward. Almost imperceptibly the change came. Quiet assurance and peace invaded his inner being, giving him renewed strength and courage. What was it his father used to say? He was struggling to remember when he felt a soft touch on his shoulder, bringing him back to his present surroundings.

Madowock had been watching over him and had sensed his wakefulness.

"Sleep," he muttered.

His last conscious thought was of his father saying, "John, the Lord will provide a way."

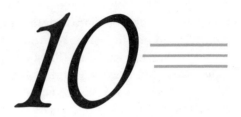

10

"MISSY, MISSY ROSA," Cally cried, hurrying through the hallway.

"In here, Cally—what is it?" Rosa called out from her room, where she was reading to Martha.

"Missy, Cally! See this!" she exclaimed, excitedly waving a scrap of paper in her hand.

"Oh, Cally—it's just a piece of paper," Rosa laughed.

"Paper talk. What paper say, Missy?"

"Well, quit waving it in the air and hand it to me," teased Rosa, taking it from her. Her hand trembled when she read the hand-printed message.

"Rosa, meet me in the rocks at noon. John."

"What paper say, Missy?"

"Here, Martha—perhaps you can finish the story by yourself," Rosa said, handing her the book.

Taking Calinta's arm, she led her into the kitchen, away from Martha's hearing, before answering.

"It's a note from John, Cally. Where did you find it?"

"By doah, right deah," Cally responded, pointing to the spot under the door. "What paper say?"

"He wants me to meet him in a secret place."

"Missy, you no can do!" Cally warned. "Cap'n in redcoat say you no leaf t' house."

"I know, Cally, but John needs me, or he wouldn't ask me to come. He'll be watching out for me. I'll take Nightstar. He can outrun any of the horses around, and certainly someone on foot."

"But, Missy . . ."

"It's settled, Cally—I must go!" Rosa interrupted, leaving her there to fret while she went to look for Shonto. He was in the stall rubbing down Nightstar.

"Shonto, when you finish the rubdown, saddle Nightstar for me. I'm going to take her out for a short run."

"All right, Missy, but . . . ," Shonto stammered, his eyes wide with wonder.

"Not now, Shonto. I've already had the same warning from Cally. Neither of you need to worry. I'll be safe."

She glanced around the barn. "Where's Mr. Worley?"

"I don' know, Missy Rosa. He left early dis mawning. He say he won't be gon' long."

"I see," Rosa said, biting her lip. She worried about the man when he left like that. She turned away.

"I'll have Nightstar ready fo' yo', Missy!" Shonto called after her.

Rosa decided to change into her riding clothes. Along with her heavy gloves and wool cape, she would be warmer.

"Cally, put some food in a sack," she asked on her way through. "He may be hungry."

When all was ready, Cally followed her all the way to the stable, wringing her hands.

"Missy . . . ," she started with tears in her eyes.

"I'll be all right, Cally," Rosa assured her, tying the lunch sack to the pommel. "Don't take on so. I'll be back before you miss me."

Leading Nightstar out the rear stable door, she mounted and rode slowly out the back way. It was farther around, but she would be away from prying eyes. Once out on the road, she rode swiftly, cutting across a field and into the bluff trail.

Lieutenant Pennington glanced at the sun. He was just

about to think his ruse would not work when he spotted her heading out the trail. "Ah," he grinned with satisfaction. He watched to make sure she would go on, then leading his horse out of the thicket, he stepped into the saddle and headed for the tavern.

"Soon you will be all mine, my dear Miss Jarden," he muttered to himself, still smarting under the reprimand he had received from Captain Mowatt. "Then we'll see who has the upper hand."

Rosa rode joyously, anticipating her meeting with John, unaware she was being observed. The wind that had come up the evening before sent gray clouds scudding across the sky. The air was brisk and cold, but she took little notice. Even the pleasure of riding Nightstar again had little effect. Her total focus was on seeing John again.

Leaving the trail to enter the trees, she guided Nightstar through the quiet forest toward the thick grove hiding the rocks. Every nerve of her body quivered expectantly as she ducked the low-hanging limbs to enter. Jumping to the ground, she led Nightstar forward toward the entrance into the rocky sanctuary. She tied the reins to a nearby bush. Nightstar reared her head and whinnied, rolling her eyes.

"Quiet, girl. It's all right. Been a long time since you've been out, huh?"

The mare reared her head again and stomped nervously. Rosa looked around the vicinity, seeing nothing unusual. Untying the bag of lunch from the saddle, she gave Nightstar a pat on the nose and entered the opening.

There was no time to cry out as rough, dark hands covered her mouth and grabbed her arms. Three Indians bound her hands and shoved her out the entrance of the rocky lair ahead of them. The hood of her cape hung low over her face, allowing her to see only the ground ahead of her. Nightstar! Where was she? When she hesitated, rough hands shoved her forward. She could hear the tread of moccasined feet behind her.

Knowing there was no use to struggle, Rosa tried to keep her wits about her. If only she had listened to Cally! But it was too late for that. Now she must use every instinct she possessed to stay alive. She refused to think about all the terrible stories she had heard. Instead, she chose to think of Martha's brave escape. She must wait and plan.

For the most part, they left her alone except to prod her around the many barriers of fallen trees and scrubby growth. It was when they came to a small ravine filled with water that she fell. Several of the braves leaped it effortlessly, but she stopped, then tried to jump, getting her feet caught in some vines along the edge. She fell half into the cold, brackish water in the bottom. Getting to her feet with her hands tied behind her was no small task. Pulling herself up the other bank, she lost her temper. Wet and disheveled, her golden hair flying, she glared at her captors.

"Why are my hands tied?" she demanded, furiously, stomping her foot. "This wouldn't have happened if my hands were free. Are you strong men afraid of a woman?"

They stared at her in surprise, then laughed. The big Indian gave a command, turning his back to walk on. Rosa felt the blade of a knife against her hand.

"Thank you—that's better," she said, turning toward her benefactor.

"Don't turn around," he whispered. "They must not know."

It was John! Rosa looked at the Indians who were walking ahead. Prodded from behind, with an order in a tongue she did not understand, she started on. It was John's voice giving the order, but it was different—more deep and resonant. Had he planned this? A light rain began to fall, and along with her wet clothes and shoes, it only added to the misery of her predicament.

With the coming of the rain the pace was increased. Rosa was just at the point she could stand no more when they entered a sheltered area. The Indians before her had already dropped to the ground. When she arrived, they paid no heed to her presence. She stood wet and miserable, wondering what to do.

John entered behind her and shoved her before him until she was under the protection of the heavy boughs of a tall evergreen tree. Gratefully, she sank to the ground, shivering in the cold. The heavy wool cape, though it was still damp, was a blessing because it broke the cold wind.

John had been leading Nightstar, and he secured the reins to a tree and proceeded to build a fire with wood that had already been gathered. Apparently, they planned to spend the night here. Well, that was all right with her. She had about reached the end of her endurance.

Her eyes followed John as he moved effortlessly about. His long, dark hair was tied back with a leather thong. He was taller, and she could see the ripple of muscles beneath the buckskin he wore from head to toe.

His stoic face did not look her direction as he worked, striking a flint to light the birch bark. He blew the tiny flame until it took hold, then carefully laid some twigs over it. Soon there was a blazing fire. The braves gathered in a circle to warm themselves, muttering among themselves in a guttural language. John joined them, sitting next to the one she had heard called Madowock.

Rosa longed to draw near to the comforting warmth of the blaze, but somehow she knew that if she did so she would be driven away. One of them, a wicked-looking fellow, glanced over at her and muttered something. They all chuckled, but she saw John stiffen ever so slightly. Hours passed with little change in activity. Rosa fought off the drowsiness that threatened to overtake her. Her legs had become numb.

Getting to her feet she walked back and forth under the dripping trees, surprised that her movement was totally ignored. Summoning more courage, she walked over to Nightstar. Placing her arms around the mare's neck, she leaned against her. The fleeting thought came to her that she could easily release Nightstar, jump onto her back, and ride away. But where could she go that she would not be found?

John must have sensed what was in her mind, for he took her roughly by the shoulders, pushing her back under the tree. "Not now—later," he whispered, shoving her to the ground. Out loud he gave her a fierce look, commanding her in the strange language of the Abenaki.

Rosa stared at the others as John returned to the fire. Seemingly, they were oblivious to what had taken place, yet she had the feeling they were aware of every move she made. John did not sit down again, but stood straight and tall in the shadow of a tree, looking very much like his Indian companions. She could feel his eyes upon her.

With sunset, the rain stopped and a mist invaded the darkening forest. To her untrained ear, the only sounds to break the stillness were the crackling of the fire and the dripping of the trees. The one called Madowock said something, gesturing with his hand. John gave a start and stepped forward, but the evil-looking one jumped to his feet in front of her.

"Do you trust this dog with one of his own kind?" he cried in his native tongue. "I will take her away!"

Madowock appeared not to have heard. Instead, he held up his hand for silence. They all listened intently, then at Madowock's quiet motion, Wypitlock returned meekly to join the circle around the fire, and it was over for the present.

Puzzled at this sudden change of behavior, Rosa looked over at John, noting he had faded farther back into the shadows. She could just barely make out his dim outline. They all appeared to be waiting expectantly, but for what? For whom?

Madowock pulled out a pipe and filled it with a small wad. Picking up a burning stick, he held it to the pipe, sending off a puff of smoke. He tossed the stick into the coals and passed the pipe to the warrior next to him.

Muffled sounds came from off in the trees. Rosa caught her breath. Could it be more Indians? Straining her ears, she thought she heard the steady tread of a horse. A quick glance at Nightstar confirmed her suspicions. The mare had her ears up looking off in the direction of the sound.

Alarmed, Rosa looked over to where John was standing, but he was gone. She tried to pierce the shadows but could not make out even a dim form. The blow of a horse announced the arrival of the rider or riders. Those in the circle around the fire continued their smoking without comment. Hurried footsteps approached the camp, and Rosa gasped as Howland Pennington strode into the light. He did not see Rosa at first because of the low-hanging boughs that partially hid her. He was carrying a heavy pouch with him, and he stopped short.

"Where's the girl?" he demanded savagely.

Madowock accepted the pipe, which had come full circle, and took a long draught before answering.

"I know you have her, for I trailed you here," Pennington attested. He dropped the bag at Madowock's feet and backed away. Madowock solemnly pointed a long arm to where the stunned Rosa sat.

Pennington whirled to face her. "You!" she cried, finally finding her voice. "You planned this! You beast!"

"Yes, I planned it, my dear Miss Jarden," he replied coolly, regaining his composure. "And after I take care of a little unfinished business, we'll be on our way."

He turned back to where Madowock and his braves sat calmly around the fire. They had not touched the pouch. This should certainly have warned him if he had been at all perceptive during his previous visits. But he was so caught up in his own desire that the change in their demeanor was lost on him.

"There—take the rest of your payment," he said in a patronizing voice, pushing it toward Madowock with the toe of his boot. "You have done well. When I get done with the girl, I may even give her to you. Ha! Ha!"

Madowock made no move, but his eyes glittered with a sinister light as he looked from one brave to the other. Pennington turned to Rosa.

"Get up from there and come with me," he ordered.

"I'd rather take my chances with the Indians," she screamed at him, retreating farther away.

"Why, you little . . . ," he ground out, ducking in to grab her by the arm. "Get out here."

As he jerked her to her feet, Rosa came kicking and fighting with all the strength she possessed. Pennington pinned her arms behind her, pulling her along. Rosa twisted and squirmed until she managed to get one hand free. She slapped him soundly by the side of the face, raking her nails to draw blood. He let her go so quickly she fell to the ground.

"You little she-devil!" he howled. "If that's the way you want it, that's the way you'll get it." He grabbed her by the hair and dragged her to him.

"Oh, dear God, please," Rosa entreated, then she stiffened, and her eyes became fixed over her shoulder.

Sensing something wrong, Pennington glanced back to see the Indians rise as one and come toward him. He dropped Rosa and reached for the gun he carried inside his coat. Backing away, he fired. Two stopped in their tracks to fall to the ground, lying there. The rest swarmed over him.

Rosa rolled to her feet and staggered toward the shadows of the trees. Pennington's hideous cries along with the bloodcurdling yells of his attackers resounded throughout the forest. The horror of it all sickened her so that she walked blindly into the grasp of strong arms. A scream died in her throat as a hand was placed over her mouth.

"Shhh. It's John. Hold steady. We must wait. There are too many of them."

"John!" she gasped, when her mouth was free. "Why did you leave me?"

"Madowock didn't want Pennington to see me. I've been here watching. I knew Pennington didn't have long to live.

Now go back to your place under the tree. I'll come for you when the time is right. Go!" His lips brushed her cheek as he turned her around, giving her a gentle push.

Reluctantly, she did as she was told, dreading the sight that awaited her. Whooping warriors, each with a bottle in his hand, were stripping the clothing from the lifeless body of Howland Pennington. Madowock was sitting on the ground, examining the pistols he had taken. Rosa averted her eyes from the gory scene.

John emerged from the darkness on the other side to dance around the prone Pennington. Laying his head back, he gave a piercing cry, joining in the merriment. Rosa could not believe her eyes. Horror-stricken at the sight and the stench of blood, she felt a sense of revulsion. She hid her face and covered her ears to blot out the scene.

The revelry went on until one by one they fell in a rum-ridden stupor to the ground. The one called Wypitlock lumbered into a tree as he stumbled backward and never moved. John fell not far from where she sat. Only Madowock remained before the fire for what seemed an eternity before he drained the last of his bottle and settled back to sleep. Shortly, the camp reverberated with the snores of the drunken Indians in exhausted slumber.

Rosa sat awake in the darkness, afraid to allow herself to drift off. The once-blazing fire was reduced to nothing but a red glow of embers when John rose silently to his feet.

Untying the reins, he led Nightstar a short distance away, returning in a few minutes for Rosa. Taking her up in his arms, he carried her to the waiting horse. Their progress was slow because of the fog, but John had taken note of the direction of the wind and headed south toward Castine.

Pale light in the eastern sky announced the beginning of a new day as John and Rosa entered the sleeping village. The exhausted Rosa had succumbed to the weariness that claimed her, reeling in the saddle, and would have fallen had John not caught her. The mare was not sturdy enough to carry the double weight, so he resorted to carrying her the rest of the way. Nightstar was content to plod along at his heels.

11

STRETCHED OUT ON HER BED, unable to sleep, Cally's heart was filled with despair and grief. Over and over, the events of the day returned to haunt her.

When Rosa had failed to return, she had walked the floor, tearfully wringing her hands. Shonto had wanted to go look for her, but she had been afraid to let him go. Why, oh why, had she allowed Miss Rosa to go? she moaned.

Mr. Worley had come in shortly after noon, and when she told him of Rosa's disappearance, he went immediately to look for her. Cally had waited in dread, not wanting to hear what she feared. Martha had begun to cry, and though Cally tried to comfort her, it had taken a long time to calm her down. Shonto had grown speechless, restlessly moving about, often pausing to stare somberly out the window.

Several agonizing hours had passed before a weary Mr. Worley returned, haggard and grim. She had fetched him a hot drink to take off the chill, searching his face for a sign of hope, but all he had done was to sadly shake his head.

"She's gone," he had managed hoarsely after several sips. "From what I could make out, and I'm no tracker, ya' understand, she went to a place up along the bluff. Her tracks led into a grove of trees near some rocks—that same one she warned me about. There were a lot of moccasin tracks there—yes sir, a

127

lot of 'em—'n' I saw her tracks mingled in with 'em, heading north. From what I could tell, they had been lying in wait to waylay her."

Taking another sip of tea, Mr. Worley had cleared his throat noisily, and continued, "Well, sir, I follered them tracks fer quite a ways, then had to give it up. She's been taken by Indians, sure enough. Too bad, too bad."

His words had fallen like hammer blows to her heart, and Cally now recalled the cold dread that had settled down upon her. Rocking back and forth with grief, she had broken down in tears. Shonto and Martha had come to her side to comfort her.

"We have one hope: She is still alive!" Worley had gone on, trying to ease her pain. "And if that bunch of Indians I saw yesterday did this, John is among them. Surely he wouldn't let anything happen to the lass, if he can help it."

"John will save her," Martha had spoken up, solemnly, her eyes grave. "He loves her. He told me so one time when I asked him. 'Sides, we can pray. That's what Father always said, and isn't that what Miss Rosa has been teaching us?"

Calinta turned her face to the wall as the child's words echoed in her head. Longtime tribal beliefs that had been a way of life for her people were hard to give up. Her troubled soul struggled with the desire to hold to her ancestral traditions, yet there was something beckoning her toward the God Elizabeth Jarden had known so well. Could it be He was real? After all, one couldn't see Him. Missy Rosa had said you have to believe with your heart that He is there, not see Him with your eyes. Calinta had watched these hardy people maintain a steady, unquestionable faith in their God through all their tragedy and heartache.

After retreating for the night and yet disturbed by her turbulent thoughts, Calinta sat up on the side of her bed. For hours she had rubbed her fetish, yet no peace had come. Frustrated and hurting, there was no place to turn for comfort. Would the white man's God hear the cry of a black woman's heart? Missy Rosa had said He would. Tears flowed down her cheeks as she remembered how she had turned away when Missy Rosa told her this. Sliding from the bed to her knees, Calinta buried her face in her hands.

"Missy Rosa's God? Do Yo' hear Calinta? I need Yo' hep. Dem Injuns has taken Missy Rosa. Don' let 'em hurt Missy Rosa. She don' no bad thin'. Calinta do wron'. Missy say Yo' hep people wha's doin' bad. Yo' hep Calinta, pleas'?"

She felt a rush of warmth throughout her body, along with a feeling of awe and wonder. A joy such as she had never experienced swept over her. No longer able to remain on her knees, Calinta stood to her feet and clapped her hands softly together.

"Does this mean Missy Rosa's coming back? Yo' is bringin' her back. Calinta know. Yo' is bringin' Missy Rosa back." She crooned, "Yo' is a biiig God! Yo' make Calinta's heart sing!"

Too excited to sleep, Calinta rested the best she could, waiting and listening to every sound. The night sped by as she relived what had just happened to her, over and over, quoting the simple scripture verses Missy Rosa had taught her.

At the first showing of gray dawn, she lit the lamp, dressing quickly. Taking up the lamp, she was about to leave for the kitchen when she noticed the fetish lying on the floor. She picked it up and stuck it in her pocket. In the kitchen, she stirred up the fire and stuck in some pitch kindling, watching until the flames licked hungrily at the wood. When it had reached sufficient flame, she pulled the fetish from her pocket and tossed it unceremoniously into the blaze.

"Don' need yo' no mo'," she mumbled, talking to herself as she replaced the hole cover. Going to the pump, she filled the teakettle and a large pot with water, placing them over the heat. "Calinta gon' t' need hot water fo' Missy Rosa, huh, God?"

A sound outside attracted her attention. She turned toward the door as muffled footsteps moved onto the porch outside. A loud thumping on the door startled her. Peering from the window, she saw what appeared to be an Indian. She called to Shonto, who came running. The urgent thumping came again, more loudly.

"Please open up in there! Hurry!"

Calinta did not recognize the voice. "Wh' fo' yo' want?"

"Please—I've got Rosa; open the door," came the answer.

Calinta gave a glad cry, turning the key in the lock. She opened the door to find standing before her a tall, buckskinned figure, with dark hair in braids held in place with a colorful headband and feathers. He was holding Rosa in his arms. Elbowing his way past the gaping Shonto and Cally, John Giles turned to ask, "Where do I take her?"

The overjoyed Calinta quickly closed the door behind him. "I show," she said, taking the lamp to lead the way to Rosa's room.

He followed to deposit Rosa gently onto her bed and tenderly pushed the hair from her pale face.

"She's not harmed," he explained, looking up to where Cally stood with questioning, worried eyes. "Mainly tired and cold. She's been through a lot. She'll be needin' some care. I'll go tend to the mare."

"Yo' no need—Shonto do," Cally said, nodding to Shonto, who hovered near the door.

John watched as Cally spread a blanket over the sleeping Rosa. Then he glanced around the room. A child was asleep on a cot in the corner. Something was familiar about the flaxen hair spread out on the pillow around the partially hidden face. The child moved restlessly at the sound of their voices and opened her eyes. Stark terror swept across her face, and John took a step backward as Martha jumped to her feet, screaming and flailing her arms.

"No! No! Go away! You're dead! No! Stay away from me!"

Calinta ran to the girl's side to quiet her. Shonto, followed by Mr. Worley, came bursting into the room. John whirled, not knowing what to expect. Worley had a gun in his hand, and he lowered it as his face lit up with recognition and gladness.

"John!" he exclaimed. "Then it *was* you I saw with them Indians! It's all right, folks—this is John Giles." He looked past him to see Rosa lying on the bed. "Aw, I see yuh brought the lass home. Thank God!" He leaned over to peer into Rosa's white face. "Is she . . . is she . . . ?"

"She's unharmed—just give out," John answered, turning a puzzled glance at Calinta, who was trying to quiet the terrified girl. "Who's this girl?"

Worley blinked at him in surprise. Well, of course—you wouldn't have known. It's Martha. She overwhelmed her captors and escaped. I found her huddled in the ruins of a burned house. She was in a bad way, so I carried her here. Miss Jarden and these people helped her and have been caring for her." He gave John an appraising glance. "The lass must hev thought yuh was an Indian. Yuh sure *look* like one."

"Martha?" John said in disbelief. He stepped to where Calinta held the distraught girl in her arms.

"Martha, it's John. Please don't be afraid."

Martha turned her head to face him. Tears filled her eyes at recognition of him, and she reached out her arms. "John, I've been praying you would come back to us!" she cried.

Clasping her tightly in his arms, John stroked her hair. "What a brave girl yu've been!" he said brokenly. Over her head, he gave Mr. Worley a questioning look. "George?"

Worley laid a warning finger over his lips, motioning with his head toward the door. John set Martha on her cot.

"You rest here, little one; we'll talk later," he promised, smiling down at her. Then he followed Mr. Worley and Shonto from the room.

John and Mr. Worley settled themselves at the kitchen table while Shonto went on to care for Nightstar.

"George?" John repeated.

Worley dropped his head, eyes focused on the toe of his boot. His thin, angular face worked with emotion as he studied how to begin.

"These hev been turrible times, lad, turrible times. I was

gone 'cross river when the Indians came that day. They got the misses and my children, same as your folk. When I arrived back, all was gone, my house burned . . . nothing left. I've already tolt yuh about finding Martha. Well, sir, when Miss Jarden found out who brought Martha here, she insisted I stay here with them and keep out of sight of that Pennington fella.

"After a few weeks, I decided t' slip back 'cross the river t' check on how the war was going. When I came back, I came 'cross an Indian war party. They had caught George, who had come back to the old homestead." He paused when Calinta entered the room to get the pan of hot water from the stove, waiting until she was gone before going on to describe the tragedy of George's last few moments of life."

Drawing a breath, he added, "Pennington was there, watching all the time."

John sat there for a long time with lowered eyes and chest heaving. When he raised his head, there was a fierce light in his eyes.

"How goes the war?"

"The last I heard, General Washington is on the march again. His men were half-starved and 'bout to give it all up at Valley Forge. Well, sir, on Christmas Eve he rallied his ragtag army and slipped across the Potomac to hit the British when they least expected it. They'd been partying and were an easy target. Since then, the Continental Army has been pushing the British back toward the sea."

"I reckon they can use some help," John said with thoughtful expression, glancing down the hall to Rosa's room.

"I've been thinking the same," Worley agreed. "That day I saw you by the river I had learned there's been a push northward to capture this British stronghold. We could probably join up with a militia by crossing the river and working our way to the south."

Further conversation on the subject was suspended as Calinta and Martha came in. Martha slipped to John's side while Calinta stirred up the fire and made some tea.

"Calinta fix yo' eats now," she announced, setting cups before them. "Missy Rosa sleepin'."

Shonto came in to take his favorite spot by the stove. "Nightstar good—eat hay now," he said, with a satisfied grin, looking from one to the other. "How Miss Rosa?"

"Sleepin'," Calinta answered.

"Somethin' *I* need to be doin'," John said wearily, "if yuh show me a place to lie down."

"I'll share my bed gladly," Worley spoke up.

John stared at the table Cally was setting. Not since he had been captured had he sat at a table and enjoyed the luxury of eating with a fork or drinking from a cup. It seemed awkward at first, much to Martha's amusement. But he soon got the hang of it again.

"Wh' yo' fin' Missy Rosa?" Calinta asked, unable to hold her curiosity any longer.

Tired as he was, John knew they had a right to know the story. Pushing back his plate, he began with his capture and the subsequent abuse he had suffered. He told of One Who Comes Running and how her love for him had changed his status. Admitting his captors had done a very good job of making an Indian out of him, he confessed to adopting their way of life rather than remaining a beast of burden. At least he was treated with more respect and even taken on hunts with them. That night of the meeting with Pennington was the first Madowock had taken him on such an excursion. When he had heard Pennington's plot to capture Rosa, he was brought back to the reality of who he was. His love for Rosa and the realization he alone could save her from a fate worse than death had brought him to understand why he had been spared. It was then he recalled again his father's dying prayer and sought God's help.

His listeners hung on his every word as he continued to relate the details of Rosa's kidnapping, Pennington's death, and their escape.

"The rest you know," he finished wearily, getting to his feet to address Worley. "Now, my friend, show me to your bed."

Rosa slept around the clock, waking late the next morning. Opening her eyes to find she was back in her own room, she lay there bewildered, trying to remember how she had gotten there.

Slowly, the horrible events still fresh in her memory came back to her. Except for her muddy cape thrown over the back of her favorite chair, which spoke eloquently, it would have seemed like a bad dream. The terrible scene there around the fire and the shrieks and cries as they danced and whirled were all very real, and John had been a part of their heathen ritual. A shudder ran through her at the remembrance of seeing him there. Yet it must have been he who had helped her escape, bringing her home to safety. Where was he now? Had he gone back to his wild life in the forest?

She threw back the covers and sat on the side of the bed. Stiff, sore muscles protested as she slid into a robe and slippers to head for the kitchen, where she heard voices. She was relieved to find Cally, Shonto, and Martha were the only ones visible. She didn't trust her feelings regarding John at this point. Their faces lit up with obvious delight as she entered.

"Yo' woked up, Missy Rosa!" Cally exclaimed. "Good! Yo' looking fin'. Sit—I fix food."

Rosa seated herself at the table, where Martha and Shonto were playing a game with straws.

"Shonto is showing me a game he played as a boy," Martha said, smiling over at her.

Rosa watched them with interest, noting the change in the girl's demeanor. Laughter came more easily, and she talked more like her former self. Rosa was sure the change had come because of John's return. Not wanting to ask about his whereabouts, Rosa asked about Mr. Worley instead.

"Shonto say he go," Cally answered, bringing her some bread and tea.

"Go?" Rosa repeated, suddenly at a loss for words.

"They went to fight the British," Martha gravely informed

her. "John said he could help General Washington's troops 'cause he knew the ways of the Indians."

Rosa was staring at her plate. Why had John left so soon? Had he seen the horror in her face and sensed her revulsion that awful night?

"He said to give yuh this."

"Wh . . . what?" Rosa responded with a start.

"He said to give yuh this," Martha repeated, handing Rosa a folded piece of paper. "I helped him write it. He had sorta forgotten how."

Rosa opened the note with trembling fingers. It was printed in bold, precise letters.

Rosa:

> I've gone to fight the war. If God spares my life, I will return. Thoughts of you were all that kept me alive during the dark hours of my life with the Indians. I must leave Martha in your care. There is no one else. I trust you will not mind. God be with you. At least now you are safe. The enemies of our land will be gone soon. I love you.

John

Without a word, Rosa folded the note and placed it by her place. She needed time to sort out her feelings. Her lack of emotion was evident to the others, who cast occasional glances in her direction. Unable to eat much, she retired to her room to dress. There were dark bruises on her arm where Pennington had grabbed her. She pushed the horror of his death quickly from her mind. At least John had been no part of his demise.

A knock at the door interrupted her thoughts. She heard Cally answer it and hurriedly brushed her hair. She was not surprised to hear Captain Mowatt's deep voice asking for her. When she put in her appearance, he was most apologetic at disturbing her, promising to take only a moment of her time.

"Cally, bring us a cup of tea," Rosa said, pointing him to a seat.

"What is it you wish to see me about?" Rosa asked, knowing full well the reason for his visit.

"My men found Lieutenant Pennington's body and this," he said, holding out a woman's glove. They followed the tracks of your horse back to Castine. Even though it is painful for you, I thought you might shed some light on what happened."

"Missy no feel good—no talk!" Calinta objected, bringing the tea. "Yo' go, come back . . ."

"It's all right, Cally," Rosa interrupted. "I'll tell Captain Mowatt what he wants to know."

She told of receiving the note and going off to the rocks, then recited the events leading to Lieutenant Pennington's death.

"How did you escape?" he asked, giving her a keen look. "There were moccasin tracks beside those of your horse. Who brought you home?"

Rosa looked him straight in the eyes and whispered, "John Giles."

He seemed startled at the name. "John Giles? I . . . I thought . . . uh, I was told all the Giles family had been massacred."

"Not all, Captain Mowatt. John and Martha were taken captive. Martha escaped and was brought here to me. I have nursed her back to health and given her a home. John was held captive and abused. We both escaped that night, and he has gone off to fight the war. George Giles ran the day of the massacre and was later caught and burned at the stake near the fort."

"Surely his death did not miss your attention, Captain," Rosa added with rancor, her brown eyes flashing. "The terrible deed was carried out on this very hill as Lieutenant Pennington looked on. Is a war to be won by the murder of innocent women and children?"

"War is not a pleasant thing, Miss Jarden," he returned defensively, unable to meet her direct gaze any longer. "Howland Pennington was a product of the war. He came from a fine family, but somewhere along the way his driving ambition sent him on the wrong path."

He gave a deep sigh, flicking a piece of dust from his coat sleeve. "Perhaps it was his belief he was destined to greatness."

"That is your opinion, Captain, and you have every right to it, but I saw the man as a conceited, ruthless killer. He brought about his own death by his insolence and his mistreatment of others."

He set his cup aside and rose to his feet, suddenly uncomfortable in her presence.

"I am sincerely grieved over what has happened to you, Miss Jarden. Please accept my apology for this outrage. I can assure you I am glad you are home safe and sound."

"Captain, you have been kind to me," Rosa said graciously, extending her hand. "Under different circumstances perhaps we could have been friends. I pray God will give you safe passage back to your homeland and your loved ones."

"Thank you," he returned, bowing low. "Good day, Miss Jarden."

"Good day, Captain."

12

ROSA LAID ASIDE the embroidery she had been working on and walked to the window. Birch and maple trees scattered among the evergreens provided a riot of red and gold in the brilliant fall sunshine. A chipmunk, with its cheek pouches stuffed with seeds, was scurrying around under the trees as if in a race for time. The crisp, frosty air of the late October mornings spoke of the change soon to come.

Nine long months had gone by since John and Mr. Worley had left to join in the battle. With the death of Howland Pennington, there had been no further forays by the Indians, who stayed far to the north. The British, feeling no longer threatened by invasion, languished in idleness and boredom, while most of the townspeople remained apart—tightlipped and cautious.

Rosa's thoughts turned to John, as they had done many times of late. At first she had been unable to deal with her unstable emotions. Every thought of him had been associated with that horrible night, reviving memories she wished to forget. How could she bring herself to compromise her Christianity by marrying a man with such heathen instincts? she had reasoned loftily.

During those early days after he had gone, Rosa had refused to acknowledge any mention of his name. Unwilling to face the issue, she had pushed it from her mind. Mercifully, with time, gradual healing had come to relieve the mental anguish of that fateful night, and she was forced to deal with her attitude toward him.

It had all come to a head when Martha, Calinta, and Shonto were discussing their predictions of John's return. Innocently, they asked Rosa when she thought he would be back.

"I don't care if that heathen ever comes back!" she had flashed back at them, fleeing before the hurt in Martha's eyes.

When Cally had come into her room later, Rosa knew the woman was upset. She had watched in amusement as Cally went about straightening the room while talking under her breath.

"Whatever it is, Cally, you might as well get it off your chest," she said finally.

Calinta had fluffed a pillow vigorously, giving it several hard slaps. Rosa had the feeling the poor pillow was getting what Cally wished she could give her charge. Dropping the pillow into a chair, Cally turned to give Rosa a stern look.

"Wh' fo' yo' say wh' yo' say?" she had demanded, hands gesturing wildly. "Mista John no say wh' you' say. Mista John says wh' yo' God."

"How do you know, Cally?—you don't say wh' God," Rosa mimicked, a little shocked at herself.

Tears had come quickly to Calinta's eyes at the caustic remark, bringing remorse to Rosa's heart. The black woman pulled up a chair near Rosa, and in her halting way told of the night God answered her prayers and the burning of the fetish, how John had prayed to God for help in rescuing Rosa, and how he had to do what he did so the Indians would not suspect him.

"Yo' say yo'sef, our God biiig God—di'nt He save yo'? I say yo' best talk wi' yo' God," Cally concluded, leaving Rosa alone to think about what she had said.

Rosa had remained motionless for a long time after Cally left the room, realizing she had been behaving like a condescending hypocrite. Her judgmental criticism of John had been wrong, and her attack on Cally had been worse.

Looking back to that day, Rosa was glad she had sought God's forgiveness. It seemed a heavy weight had been removed from her heart. Peace and healing had come to her troubled soul. She longed for the time when she could see John again to let him know how she felt. But these many months she had heard no word from him or her father.

She crossed to the window looking out over the bay. The fog bank that so often closed in on the harbor had been pushed far out to sea, and the water sparkled in the morning sun. A ship bearing the British flag was making its way into the harbor.

Long before now she had hoped the British would give up their stranglehold on the area and sail away. But as yet they still seemed deeply entrenched. As long as they held on, there was little hope of seeing her father again. She turned away with a long sigh.

Martha looked up from the book she was reading. "Is something wrong?"

"No, dear; I guess I'm just restless—that's all," Rosa responded. "Father has been on my mind of late. It's been a long time since I've heard from him."

Watching the ship's progress, it suddenly struck her that there were more than the usual supply ships at anchor in the bay. The boat coming in was a transport, and when she looked more closely she spotted others, along with several frigates, all heavily armed. What could this mean? Were they massing for an attack on the American positions?

"Martha, get Shonto and Cally!"

When they came running, she pointed to the boats.

"What do you make of this?"

As they watched the transport gain the harbor, still another was emerging from the mist.

"We can see better from Father's room," Rosa suggested, leading the way up the stairs.

They watched in awe as British ships, with colors unfurled, filled the harbor. What a majestic sight! Soldiers began pouring from their quarters, pointing and shouting. Some were throwing their hats into the air. Rosa saw Captain Mowatt come from his headquarters down at Mullet House with some of his men. They strode down to the water's edge. A small dinghy put out from one of the foremost frigates and made its way to the shore where Mowatt stood. Rosa looked for the small telescope her father kept nearby, but it was gone, taken by the British soldiers, no doubt. From what Rosa could tell, a man stepped ashore and handed Captain Mowatt something.

His actions led Rosa to believe it was a message of some kind. He turned and gave an order to one of his men, and the messenger returned to his ship. So began the withdrawal of the British from Castine. For several days the beating of the drums escorted uniformed men in an orderly fashion to waiting transports.

To the hopeful residents of Castine, it appeared the British were moving out. Could it mean the war was over and they would be free? Some hardy souls ventured into the streets to watch in silence, while others remained behind closed doors, peering out between the shutters.

When the ruffle of drums and the sound of marching men had died away, there was an empty calm in the village. One by one, the ships set their sails and glided from the harbor.

Though some of the cheering townspeople had gathered at the shore to celebrate their freedom, Rosa refrained from joining them, going out only into the yard. Up to now, she had not known who was a friend. Since it had been rumored her father was a spy, the women of the village had stayed to themselves for fear of reprisal.

"If only Papa and Mama could be here to see this!" Martha said wistfully.

Rosa put her arm around the girl to lead her back into the house. "They did not die in vain, Martha. They will long be remembered for their sacrifice. Because of brave people like them, our land is free. Your father and mother would be proud to know that you will grow up, marry, and bear children to carry on their dreams in a free land." She brushed the tears from Martha's cheeks. "We're facing a new beginning. Soon John will be back, and we'll be a family."

Speaking with more assurance than she felt in her heart, Rosa left to go to her room. Throwing herself across the bed, she wept quietly—not for herself, this time, but for all those who had given their lives for this moment. Was John one of them? No, her heart denied hotly!

"Dear God, Your Word is true," she whispered. "I've had only Your promises to lean on these many months. Help me to be strong a little while longer and believe You'll bring John and Father back to me."

"Missy Rosa, Missy Rosa!" Shonto called through the door.

"What is it, Shonto?" Rosa answered, drying her tears on the coverlet.

"Missy Rosa, come 'n' see!"

Rosa opened the door to find Shonto so excited he could hardly stand still. His face was beaming, and he beckoned for her to come with him. Following him into the side yard, she saw her father's horse tied to a tree. He looked gaunt and tired.

"Oh, Charger, what have they done to you?" she cried, running toward him.

The stallion shied away from her, rolling his eyes and snorting with fear. Rosa stopped in her tracks.

"Shonto, he doesn't know me anymore. See if you can approach him."

Slowly, Shonto moved toward the large horse, crooning softly, but Charger only backed away, rearing his magnificent head. Closer and closer, Shonto moved in until he was able to reach for the halter. He laid a hand on Charger's forehead, still cajoling and coaxing. The big animal trembled as he accepted the gentle, caressing touch of Shonto's hand.

"Missy, open door," he said in a low voice.

Rosa hastened to obey, waiting anxiously inside until the horse was safely in his stall. Nightstar whinnied a greeting.

"Don't yo' worry none, Missy Rosa. He gonna be fine now. We'll feed 'n' rest 'im, 'n' he'll come along."

"I know, Shonto—he always loved you. At least they didn't break his wonderful spirit."

The days sped by, and times were hard for the people of Castine. The British had taken everything of value with them, leaving little for the people who scavenged the empty buildings and fort. Faced with the prospects of a hard winter, they looked longingly to the sea for returning merchant ships.

With Martha's help, Rosa made a list of their meager supplies. There would not be enough food to carry them through the long winter months. Free to fish in the harbor once more, Shonto had set lobster traps and began fishing. His catch was prepared and hung to dry. The precious meat would go along with the few ears of corn he had hidden and carefully guarded from the British. Deer were plentiful, but there were no guns or ammunition with which to hunt. Shonto had fashioned a spear, but as yet he had not had any luck in killing one of the illusive animals.

What hay Shonto had found and hauled home for the horses would have to be rationed out. Until the snow came, Shonto was grazing the horses outside to help preserve the supply. In taking inventory of the situation, Rosa noted that getting in an adequate amount of firewood for heat would be a priority.

On the first clear, crisp fall day that presented itself, Shonto cut trees and split the wood, while Rosa, Calinta, and Martha, midst a lot of lighthearted teasing, carried it into the barn, neatly stacking it.

None of them took note of the tall figure coming toward them through the woods with soft tread. Martha tripped over a stick of wood and went sprawling into the brightly colored leaves covering the ground, becoming the object of much laughter. The man stepped behind a tree to watch the merriment, undetected, chuckling to himself.

Rosa, her golden hair flying in the air, was a picture as she gathered up an armload of leaves to shower down onto the giggling, squirming girl. Cally came from the barn to watch the fun. She was the only one facing him, and he laid a warning finger to his lips as he stepped from his covert to stride noiselessly toward the girls.

Cally returned her knowing gaze to Rosa's radiant face in anticipation of the surprise. Martha had gained her feet and was gathering an armload of leaves to fight back. Rosa turned to evade the threat, running right into the arms of the man.

"Oh!" she cried, trying to free herself from his strong grasp.

"John, John—you're home!" Martha yelled joyously, dropping the leaves to run to him.

"I shore am, little one," John responded warmly. "I'm here to stay. The war is over. The British surrendered at Yorktown."

Holding on to Rosa with one arm, John scooped his sister up in the other, holding her close, but his questioning gaze searched Rosa's face.

Once over her shock, Rosa could only stare up at him in wondrous relief. He seemed older, and there were tired lines creasing his cheeks. The long, dark hair she remembered was shorter now under the brown, broad-brimmed hat he wore. He was still dressed in buckskin smelling of the forest and campfire, but it was such as the pioneers wore. She could hear the rapid beating of his heart, and her own answered in unsteady response.

"John, I . . . I'm so happy you are back," she whispered, clinging to him. "I've prayed for this day."

She heard his sudden intake of breath and felt his arm tighten around her. A light glowed in his gray eyes, so like Martha's. Keeping his hold on them both, he led them to where Calinta and Shonto stood waiting with broad smiles.

"Mista John, yo' home!—'at's good!" Cally exclaimed, clapping her hands.

"Calinta, I see yuh've been takin' good care of these girls," John said, pushing Martha and Rosa gently forward. "Now, if yuh'll take 'em in the house, Shonto 'n' I will finish up this job."

Following Calinta into the house, Rosa looked back to see John had already laid his jacket aside and was wielding the axe with sure, powerful strokes, sending the chips flying. Her heart was full, and she drew comfort from his presence.

Her offer to help with the evening meal was turned down by Cally, who teased, "Yo' best be prettying yo'sef. God don' sent yo' man back." Red of face, Rosa fled the room, glad for the opportunity to have a private moment to reflect on what she would to say to John.

Once inside her room, she bathed her face in cold water and dried it while surveying herself in the mirror. Sober eyes gazed back at her as she faced the realization this was her time of reckoning.

Although John had been happy to see her, Rosa knew she must not read any more into his return than just that. After all, it was only natural he would come back to Castine for Martha. He had been gone a long time, and his feelings for her could have changed. However, that thought was not one she wished to dwell on.

Rosa changed her dress, then lingered long in her room, dreading to face John. One moment she was ecstatic as she recalled the tightening of his arm around her and the warm glow in his eyes. The next, assailing doubts and fears put a damper on her happiness. By the time Cally sent Martha to call her to supper, Rosa's stomach was in knots, but there was no escaping the inevitable.

John was just coming into the kitchen from the barn when Rosa put in her appearance. She avoided his probing glance, claiming her seat at the table. Rosa stammered a prayer of thanksgiving, then listened quietly while Martha chattered happily, with occasional comments from Shonto and Cally filling in the few gaps in conversation.

Anxious to hear about the war, the three of them prevailed upon John to tell his story. While he talked, Rosa could feel his eyes on her face. When he fell silent, Shonto asked the question that was on all their minds.

"Wh' happenin' to Mista Worley? Is he gon' t' be comin' back?"

"I don't think so, Shonto," he answered slowly with furrowed brow, pushing back his plate. "The last time I saw him, he said he didn't have anything to come back to."

"Now if the rest of you will excuse us, I would like for Rosa to take a walk with me," he continued, getting to his feet.

Startled, Rosa finally forced herself to meet his puzzled gaze.

"I'll get a shawl," she murmured, leaving her unfinished plate of food to go to her room.

The sun was low in the sky as they made their way down the hill toward the harbor.

"You were awfully quiet at the table, Rosa. Is somethin' wrong?"

"No, I was just thinking," was her evasive answer.

"About what?" he pressed.

"Uh, about what happened after you left," Rosa replied, avoiding the direct truth.

Instead, she told him of Captain Mowatt's visit and the withdrawal of the British troops, falling silent when they reached the shore to stand mutely watching the red rays of the setting sun play upon the water. The bay, once filled with activity, lay empty and still, interrupted only by the sound of waves lapping at the rocky shore and the cry of a gull, looking hopefully for a handout.

"Every day since the British left, we have looked for the merchant ships to come. The soldiers took everything, even stole Father's guns when they searched his room. We are desperately in need of supplies here." When John made no comment, she added wistfully, "Father should sail in any day now."

John took her by the shoulders, gently turning her to face him. "That's what I wanted to talk to you about, Rosa," he began, his voice failing him under her steady gaze.

Tears sprang to Rosa's brown eyes, and she leaned her golden head against his chest, waiting for the words she did not wish to hear. His arms came up to hold her close as he related the story.

"While I was in Boston tryin' to catch a boat up this way, I overheard a captain tellin' about bein' caught in a great storm just three days off the coast. His ship had taken on a lot of water, but he made it in. Another ship within view wasn't so fortunate and went down. I asked him if he knew who the captain was." He paused, wishing there was anything else he could say but what he had to tell her.

Rosa held her breath as he continued.

"He . . . he said it was a man from Castine by the name of Jarden."

Rosa remained motionless for a full moment, then turned her face toward the sea. Out there somewhere was her father, and her faith in a merciful God refused to let her believe he was dead.

"I'm glad it was you who told me, John," she said presently. "The night I said good-bye to Father, I was afraid I would never see him again, but now, somehow, I feel in my heart he will come back someday."

"Rosa," John whispered tenderly, placing his finger under her chin to turn her face up to his, "I love you. I want to marry you and take care of you if you will have me."

"Shhh," she whispered, placing a trembling finger on his lips. "I have something to say to you first.

"When you left, I wasn't sure about my love for you. Seeing you there that awful night dancing like a bloodthirsty heathen repulsed and confused me. You seemed so . . . so different . . . so like an Indian . . . it frightened me. I became narrow and judgmental, unable to see beyond that night. My faith in you was shaken, but Cally showed me where I was wrong. You had risked your life to save me from a terrible fate, and I was a wretched, ungrateful, 'better than thou' woman." She paused, taking a deep breath. "I guess what I'm trying to say is . . . will you forgive me?"

His hands fell to his side, and he took a step backward, his face paling in the dim light.

"There's nothing to forgive. I . . . I love you," he choked out, gazing at the ground beneath his feet.

Rosa felt she was standing on the edge of a precipice, about to fling herself headlong over it. Her love broke its bonds as she looked into his face with shining eyes.

"John, look at me," she said tremulously, waiting until he had turned his troubled eyes back to hers. "I don't love you like I did then. When I realized what I had done, I was desperate. Not knowing if you would want to come back, I prayed God would bring you back to me. Even in my darkest night of despair, He put a song in my heart and gave the courage to go on each day."

Rosa pressed her trembling hand to her heart, savoring the moment. Then, taking a deep breath, she plunged on.

"I don't love you like I did then. I love you as only a woman can love a man . . . with all my heart. Yes . . . John, yes. I will be your wife."

Even though Rosa had dreamed of this moment, she was not prepared for his joyous response. With a strangled cry, he swept her up in his arms and held her close.

"My darling Rosa. Through all these terrible times, it has been your love that has given me hope and a reason for living! I will never leave you again!"

Standing arm in arm with rapt expression, they watched the last orange glow of the sun fade from the harbor before turning to walk slowly up the hill.

"When will we be married, Rosa? I don't mean to press you, dear, but I hope it will be soon."

"Christmas Day," she answered dreamily. "Yes, it'll be Christmas Day. I've always thought it would be nice to be married on Christmas Day. It is the day of new beginnings."

"That'll be good," John replied, squeezing her hand. "With Shonto's help, there will be time to clear the land and begin buildin' us a home—unless, of course, you prefer to remain here."

Looking up at the street at the white-pillared house, a pained expression fleetingly crossed her face. "It's the only home I have ever known, but it is Father's. We will stay until Father comes home, for Cally and Shonto's sake.

"Besides, dear husband to be," she went on, her voice taking on a lighter tone, "whither thou goest, I will go." Blushing, she hid her face against his shoulder.

Inside the house, two sets of dark eyes had been anxiously watching their approach. Witnessing the couple's final embrace, two dark faces broke into broad, happy smiles.

13

CANNON FIRE EXPLODED, rocking the ship and arousing from his stupor the man lying chained to the wall in the hold. The ship came alive with the excited cries of the pirate horde caught unaware, and feet pounded along the deck over his head as the motley crew ran to meet the challenge of an attack. Another cannonball hit the ship, penetrating just above the water line. Debris fell around the prisoner, who strained futilely at his shackles. Boarding ropes were thrown. He heard the clank of the hooks as they took hold and the scuffling up the sides of the vessel as the attackers scrambled aboard. Cries of pain could be heard amid the shouting. After a while, the light was blocked as someone came below. "What do yo' mean gettin' me down in this stink hole? This better be important!"

"Aye, it is, Captain—look!" The sailor pointed a finger at him.

"Bring a light!" the captain ordered, peering into the gloom.

A lantern was quickly produced, and the captain held it above where the man lay.

Unfearing dark eyes glared up at him from a face surrounded by an unkempt beard and shaggy dark hair. The tattered coat he wore was of the common style worn by the men who commanded ships. What was left of the trousers revealed bare legs and feet, full of sores.

"Who are you, and what are you doing here?" he was asked.

"That, sir, depends . . . on who I'm . . . talking to," was the weak answer.

"By ye saints! Don't you know I have the power to have you run through with the sword or left here to go down with the ship?"

"That . . . I do, sir."

"Then who are you?"

"I am . . . Captain . . . Matthew . . . Jarden, once captain of the . . . *Surgosa Rose,* more recently the . . . *Sea Mist.* My ship was hit by a violent storm, went down in a gale . . . can't account for the rest of my crew . . . God rest their souls . . . ordered them to abandon ship . . . the boat broke apart . . . I clung to part of the hull . . . pirates found me . . . holding for ransom."

"Loosen his irons," the captain commanded.

The sailor by his side jumped to obey the order.

"Help him to his feet."

Jarden found his legs unwilling to hold his body after long weeks of inactivity and little food. They buckled beneath him.

"Get somebody to help you get him up on deck!" he thundered.

"How long since you've had food, Jarden?" he asked, turning back to the weakened man.

"I . . . I don't rightly know, sir."

The captain stepped back as three husky men came down to lift Jarden into the fresh air. "Take him to quarters on our ship. Careful now—he's weak. Don't drop him!"

He turned to the circle of men standing around him. "Are we finished here? Did you get rid of all the shark bait?"

"Aye, we did, sir," a burly young sailor replied.

"Then send this rat-infested, stench-filled vermin floater to the bottom, and get back aboard ship," he boomed. "We'd best be settin' our sails for the open seas. There may be other pirate frigates around, and they mightn't be as easy to overrun."

Two weeks later, Matthew Jarden lay on his hard bed resting. Since being brought aboard the *Sea Nymph,* commanded by Captain Benjamin Stroud, he had been treated well. A bath and decent clothing had been provided, along with food regularly brought to him until he had gained sufficient strength to make it to the galley on his own. The sores on his limbs had been treated and were somewhat better.

Now on the mend, he tried to piece together the time lost while in chains. With the astute eyes of a seaman, he noted the oblique rays of the sun. It was located far into its march toward the winter solstice.

"Matey, could you tell me what month this is?" he asked of a man who came by.

The man scratched the stubble of beard on his chin, twisting his face up in thought.

"The way I reckon, Cap'n, it be along toward the 'leventh month of the year," the mate answered, hurrying on his way.

Left to himself, Captain Jarden's thoughts went to Rosa. He had hoped to be home for the holidays. The gifts he was bringing for them had gone down with the ship. Realizing the time was growing late and having no idea where he was being taken, he closed his eyes. Disappointed though he was, Captain Jarden was grateful to be able to get home at all.

A shadow blocked the light of the window, and he opened his eyes to see Captain Stroud standing over him. It was the first he had seen him since being brought aboard, although he had heard his voice giving orders.

"Thought you were asleep," he greeted Jarden amiably, pulling the stump of a pipe from his pocket. "I see you are looking better. Good! Is there anything I can do for you?"

Jarden studied his rescuer's face, noting the strong set of the jaw surrounded by a mop of prematurely gray beard. He judged the man to be about his own age, in his early 50s.

Piercing, gray eyes under shaggy brows returned his steady gaze as the captain sent puffs of smoke rolling upward. He leaned against a post, waiting for Jarden to speak.

"Yes, if I may ask, where are we, and where are you going? It seems I've lost track of time and have no idea where I am. A mate told me what month it is, but I didn't ask our location."

"Well, right now we are about three days out of Boston, where I'll be picking up cargo to carry north to Castine Harbor. I hear the British are gone now, and if I know anything about them blasted Tories, those folk up that way are going to be needing food and supplies."

Captain Jarden felt his eyes grow misty. "By the Lord Almighty!" he exclaimed. "What providence He has bestowed on me! Captain Stroud, would it be possible to gain passage with you to Castine? That is my home, and I have a daughter there. The last time I put in to Castine Harbor, it was to bury my wife. I barely escaped arrest by the British and made it safely out, but I had to leave Rosa there. I need to go back to see about her. I have no money now, but I'm willing to work for passage."

"You'll do nothing of the like," Captain Stroud assured him, taking his pipe from his mouth. "I have family waiting for me in Boston. When we put in there, we'll get you medical help, and you can rest and regain your strength while the ship is taking on cargo. Well, I'd best be getting back to quarters. Good day, Captain."

"Good day, sir."

After he had gone, Captain Jarden bowed his head in recognition of God's great hand in the affairs of his life. Just a few short days ago he despaired of ever seeing Rosa again. Now he felt his heart swell with renewed hope that he might return to Castine soon.

While in Boston, he would go see his old friend Captain Charles Fenton. Perhaps Fenton would arrange a loan until he was commissioned to another ship. His mind went to the woman he had met on his last visit in Boston. She had come sweeping into Fenton's drawing room, radiant and excited. Dressed in a full-skirted brown dress that accented her fair face, framed by rich auburn hair escaping from the matching bonnet she wore, she presented a pretty picture of grace and beauty.

"Oh, forgive me, Cousin Charles," she had apologized upon seeing Jarden sitting there. "I didn't know you had someone here."

Both men had stood to their feet. "It's quite all right, Mary; this is Captain Jarden from up Castine way. We were just having a friendly chat. What is it you wish to see me about?"

"I am having a small dinner party tonight and wondered if you could come," she had informed Fenton.

"You're not up to your game of matchmaking again, are you, Mary?" Fenton, who like Jarden was a widower, had countered, trying to appear stern.

"How can you say such a thing, Charles?" she had pouted prettily. "For your information, there will be other men there to entertain the ladies. Perhaps even Captain Jarden will join us," she had added saucily, turning merry brown eyes on him. Intrigued by her beauty, the captain had somehow stammered his acceptance.

"Good!—then it is settled," she had smiled, showing an even row of white teeth. "I will expect both of you handsome gentlemen at eight." With that she had gone, leaving both men to ponder the whirlwind who had just engulfed them.

Thinking of her now, Captain Jarden wondered if he would see her again. He had been taken by her warmth and quick wit and had found himself thinking of her often during the lonely hours at sea.

Boston Harbor was alive with activity when the *Sea Nymph* put in. In the months following the end of the war, commerce had been freely flowing in and out of the port in spite of the continuing threat of piracy on the high seas. Most successful ships were well armed and manned with capable fighting crews, making piracy more difficult. The *Sea Nymph,* commanded by Captain Stroud, was one such ship. While he waited to go ashore with Stroud, Jarden took in the trim ship with a practiced, admiring eye. It was built larger and stronger than any he had sailed. When he commented on it to Captain Stroud, the man assured him it *should* be—it had been built up the Penobscot River in Bucksport.

"No finer timber to build ships anywhere than that from up that way," he declared, leading the way to the wharf. "The house is but a short way. We can walk if you are up to it."

"The walk would be good. Would you happen to know Captain Charles Fenton?" Jarden asked, thinking of Mary.

"That I do, sir. Why do you ask?"

"Captain Fenton is a longtime friend of mine. I thought I would drop by to see him while I'm here."

"Good man—we are related," Stroud returned.

The rest of the way they talked of mutual friends and the change that had come about in the business of shipping. Captain Jarden found in Captain Stroud a vast source of information. "What you ought to do, Captain, is provide your own ship, and the money from the cargo will be all yours," Stroud advised.

"That is what I did, until I lost the *Surgosa Rose*," Jarden explained. "Right successful at it, too, if I may say so. Been trying to get on my feet ever since. Would have been in fine shape if the *Sea Mist* hadn't gotten taken by the storm. I think it had a structural problem, to break up like it did."

"Well, here we are," Captain Stroud announced, opening a tall gate, waiting to allow his guest to enter the courtyard.

Once in, Captain Jarden waited on his host to precede him to the door. They entered into a spacious hall running through the entire length of the house. Doors led into rooms on each side. A spiral stairway to the left apparently led to a second story. Captain Jarden heard rapid footsteps overhead and then a glad cry as a woman descended the stairs.

"Husband, you're home! Oh, it is good you're here!"

Her questioning black eyes fell on Jarden, standing in the background. Benjamin Stroud took her hands, drawing her forward to meet him.

"Wife, this is Captain Matthew Jarden. We rescued him

from a certain death. He will need medical attention and a good rest. Captain, my wife, Nina Marguerita. She is of Spanish descent and has a fiery nature—ha, ha—but don't let that fool you. She has a heart of gold."

Mrs. Stroud was a handsome woman who wore her hair drawn back from her regal face. White skin accented the darkness of her eyes, and her smile was genuine.

Captain Jarden bowed low and took the hand she offered. "Mrs. Stroud, I am honored."

"I show you to room, señor," she greeted him warmly. "Come."

Stroud went into the drawing room, leaving Captain Jarden to follow Mrs. Stroud up the stairs. She walked with a sweeping grace, head held high. He was shown to a large, airy room with windows overlooking the harbor. The bed looked inviting.

"I send someone to help with bath," she said with halting English, leaving him there.

A small room containing a washbowl, pitcher, and iron bathtub opened off the main part. Feeling very tired, the captain lowered his weary frame into a chair. It was there a man servant found him. After a hot bath, a salve was applied to the remaining sores on his legs, and he was helped to bed. The walk up the hill had taken its toll, and he was soon asleep.

Several days later, he was reading in the drawing room when he heard a familiar voice in the hall outside. Mary Hinton came bursting into the room.

"Aw, there you are, Captain Jarden. My brother stopped by today and told me you were here. He said you needed cheering up, and from the looks of you, I agree." She laughed. "You poor dear—what a terrible ordeal you've been through! Thanks be to our Maker and to my brother's bravery, you are alive."

"It is good to see you, Miss Hinton," he returned, a little chagrined he had been the object of their discussion. "I apologize for my appearance."

Mrs. Stroud brought in some tea, leaving Mary to serve. She stayed for an hour, chatting vivaciously about events in Boston. The time went quickly, and after she had gone it seemed the sun had gone behind a cloud.

Retiring to his room, Captain Jarden found himself thinking about her. Not since his wife had died had he met such a charming woman. She made a man feel happy she was there with him.

Several days later, during the evening meal, her name came up several times. For whatever reason, Captain Jarden did not try to analyze as he listened with interest to conversation involving her name.

Benjamin Stroud finished the last bite of his mincemeat pie and laid aside his napkin. Mrs. Stroud excused herself, becoming discreetly absent.

Stroud waited respectfully for his guest to finish his food, then clearing his throat noisily, he began.

"I went to see Charles Fenton today. He sends his best regards and wanted me to tell you he was sorry for your misfortune and would drop by to see you tomorrow. Come—let's go into the drawing room."

When they had settled themselves comfortably, Captain Jarden waited for his host to speak. It was obvious he had something on his mind besides a social call on Fenton. He lit his pipe with a thoughtful air, then held it in his hand.

"Captain Fenton tells me you are a good seaman . . . in fact, among the best. In recognition of this, we have both decided, along with a silent partner, to advance you a loan for a ship when you are ready. You can make payment with each shipment of cargo. Does that sound fair to you?"

Captain Jarden sat stunned. What he had just heard was beyond his fondest dreams. Finding his tongue, he assured Captain Stroud it was more than fair.

"I can assure you, sir, your confidence in me will be unshaken."

"Good. I have had another ship ordered from Bucksport

for some time. It should be ready soon. You may take its purchase. By the time you get it outfitted and find a top-notch crew, you should be ready to go back to the sea."

Stroud got to his feet and walked to the door. "If you'll excuse me, I have some log work to finish. Make yourself comfortable. Oh, by the way, Mary has invited you to dine with her tomorrow evening. You will go?"

"Yes, I will go," Captain Jarden found himself saying.

Shortly, he retired to his room and stretched out on the bed. His last conscious thought was of merry brown eyes and infectious laughter.

He awoke the next morning to a leaden sky and light rain. By noon the rain had increased, and he wondered how he would get to Mary Hinton's that evening. All afternoon the rain pounded against the windowpanes. The whole day had been depressing, and he found it hard to concentrate on the book he was reading. Laying it aside, he sat staring at the fire in the grate.

It was in such a state that Charles Fenton found him. Jarden was glad to see his old friend. A servant brought tea, and they talked long. When it came time to go, Fenton stood and looked down at him.

"Mary tells me you are coming to supper. She invited me also, but I have another engagement. However, I am sending my carriage over to take you there. The weather is too bad for anyone on foot." Captain Fenton gave his friend an appraising look. "Especially one in your condition. I trust you will enjoy yourself. Mary is good company."

After he had gone, Captain Jarden scowled, wondering how many others in Boston knew he was dining with Mary Hinton tonight. Picturing himself there with her brought to mind his lack of decent clothes to wear. A glance at the darkening sky made him realize it was useless to send a servant for clothing this late.

"Oh well—I'll just not be able to go," he sighed, mounting the stairs. "When the driver comes, I'll send a message with him."

In his room he found the lamps had been lit, adding a warm, cheerful atmosphere. A fire in the grate was welcomed to chase away the cold November chill.

Much to his surprise, he found a handsome new outfit had been laid out on his bed, complete with a captain's hat. Almost for certain, it had been the thoughtfulness of Charles Fenton. Jarden felt a rush of feeling for this kind man.

That happy evening spent with Mary Hinton became the first of many. The day Captain Stroud announced he would be sailing soon, Matthew Jarden knew he would have to deal with his feelings for her. That very evening he asked Mary to become his wife, and she readily accepted, much to the delight of all. The wedding was set for his next return to Boston.

However, his happiness was blemished by the prospect of his return to Castine and what he would find there. The last word he had received of Rosa's welfare had been from the captain who had taken his message to her. Though the man had returned with a favorable report, later news of the rout of the Continental forces by the British and the subsequent Indian raids and massacres had been troubling.

Now, faced with his probable return, old fears he had refused to ponder returned to haunt him. Would his home still be there, or had it been burned to the ground with the others? If the house was intact, there would be the lingering presence of Elizabeth Jarden to deal with. Deciding it was not fair to bring his new bride to live there, he vowed to leave it all to Rosa. It was best to start anew.

A few days before they were to sail, Captain Jarden was in the drawing room reading. A rap on the door summoned a servant to answer. From where he sat, he heard a man's voice.

"Is this the residence of Cap'n Stroud?"

"Yessuh," was the answer.

"Well, I've been told a Cap'n Jarden was stayin' here. Is he in?"

"Yessuh. You come in, please?"

Captain Jarden laid his book aside and stepped into the hall. A man with a tired, angular face, dressed in the attire of a farmer, was standing just inside the door. The servant retired to another part of the house.

"I am Captain Jarden. What did you wish to see me about?" Jarden asked, searching his mind for the man's identity.

"I heard talk down at the docks about a sea cap'n's rescue, 'n' I asked 'em who it be," the man answered. "They said Cap'n Stroud would know. So I hunted him up. He had a right to his suspicions and said, 'Who want t' know?' Well, sir, I told him I had a message fer Cap'n Jarden from Castine. He told me how to find yuh."

"What is your message, Mister?"

"Name's Worley, sir, and it's a long story," the man informed him, looking past him into the drawing room.

"Come in, Mr. Worley," Jarden instructed, leading the way.

"It's 'bout yer family," Worley started, after seating himself in an opposite chair. "I thought you'd want t' know what happened t' 'em."

Captain Jarden gave a start, and his blood ran cold.

"Speak, man!" he cried hoarsely, leaning forward in his chair. "In the name of God, be quick about it!"

Thus, for the next hour, Mr. Worley related in detail all that had taken place during the captain's absence. While he listened, Rosa's father found himself experiencing the total gamut of emotions. As the story unfolded, he laughed, cried, became angry, and was filled with pride for his offspring.

"Well, sir, if it hadn't been fer John Giles' love fer the lass, she'd 've suffered a sad fate. Heard tell from someone up there that they're gettin' married Christmas Day.

"That's one spunky girl yuh hev there, Cap'n. She done yuh proud handlin' them Tories. They don't come any better. I'm mighty grateful fer what she did to save my life.

"I guess that be all," Worley said with finality, getting to his feet.

"Thank you, Mr. Worley—your concern is appreciated," Jarden said, returning to the hall with him. "I was fearful of what may have happened to them when I heard all the heart-breaking stories from up that way."

"By the way, Mr. Worley, what are you doing now?"

"Since the war ended, I've been lookin' fer work down this way. Don't have nothin' t' go back there fer."

"Would you like to work for me on my ship?"

"Haven't been on the sea since I married the missus, sir."

"I want a loyal mate I can totally depend on; it'll all come back to you," Captain Jarden said hopefully.

"I'll be loyal, sir," Worley returned with feeling. "Yuh can count on that."

"Good! I'm going back to Castine soon and will pick up my ship at Bucksport. You'll probably need some sort of income while you're waiting. I'll make arrangements with Captain Fenton so that you can draw half pay until I return." The captain recognizing the tattered coat and worn-out boots as other evidence of Rosa's generosity.

"I'm thankin' yuh, Cap'n, 'n' I'll be waitin'. Sometimes I can pick up little jobs around the docks. If I get in a bind, I'll see your Cap'n Fenton. Give my regards to the lass, sir. Good day t' yuh."

"Good day, Mr. Worley."

Three days later, the sturdy ship made its way out of the Boston Harbor toward the open sea. Captain Jarden stood near the main spar with mixed emotions. Behind, he had left the woman he loved, with the promise to return soon so that they could be married. Ahead lay the anticipation of seeing Rosa, Cally, and Shonto. He knew Mary would be safe among friends, but his family in Castine was foremost in his mind at the moment.

Mr. Worley had indicated they had been having a struggle since their stores had been confiscated. Surely the merchant ships had begun arriving, yet Captain Stroud had alluded that he might be the first to go. Did that mean the British had been slow in giving up their stranglehold on the area?

He thought of what Worley had said about John Giles. That would be Tom Giles' eldest son, the one who had come to the grave that day. Good-looking boy. So Rosa had chosen to marry him. Somehow he had hoped she would marry a seafaring man. No matter. If she was happy, he would be happy.

Once free of the harbor, the *Sea Nymph* was turned northward with its sails fully extended. The gentle swells broke across the prow with a familiar swooshing noise, raising and lowering the boat in a steady rhythm all familiar to Matthew Jarden. A man of the sea since he had first sailed aboard his father's ship, he always thrilled to the sound. Benjamin Stroud came to stand by his side, and the two of them sensed a kindred spirit, staring out across the open water.

"Captain, will yours be the first ship to enter the harbor of Castine?"

"Aye, far as I know 'tis true. The British weren't in a hurry to give up their hold on the area. But I heard the crown felt like it wasn't worth the effort anymore, so they pulled them out. Guess it has something to do with the mix they're in over in India. When they pulled out recently, they took everything with them, leaving those poor people to face a hard winter without food and oil. Most merchant ships refused to go, since there was little chance of money for their cargo. Don't know when I'll ever get my pay, but someone had to get help to them."

The compassion of the man touched Captain Jarden deeply, and he could not speak for a moment. Had he not seen the same goodness in Mary? What a fortunate man he was to have such a friend!

"Did Captain Fenton tell you of my hauling arms to supply the Continental Army?" he asked, finally.

"That he did not," Stroud replied, "but I'm glad you told me, for I did the same. The risk was great, but it was worth it!

Running the gauntlet of British ships was no easy task. Had it not been for the speed of the *Sea Nymph,* I may not be here to tell the story."

"Tell me of this daughter of yours," he added, changing the subject.

"Rosa? Rosa takes after her mother in beauty—but has more inner fire and strength. In that respect she is like me. Although womanlike, she prefers a home rather than the sea. I realized it was dangerous to leave her there with Cally and Shonto, but I felt it was more dangerous to take her with me. To me, she seemed such a slip of a girl in a man's world. Little did I know how smart and resourceful she was. I could only trust the honor of the British officers and pray she would make it through the war unharmed."

"Aye, if she had the blood of her father flowing in her veins, she probably did," Captain Stroud observed. "Wouldn't the patriots there have come to her aid?"

"That, my friend, is highly unlikely, since I was branded a British spy to cover their embarrassment at my escape. My only hope was in God's providence. When I was a prisoner in despair of my life, all hope had fled. But just as God sent you to my rescue, I now know He sent someone to help Rosa. A man by the name of Worley came to me with word of her the other day. It was a hair-raising story."

"Come to my quarters. I want to hear of this."

It was late afternoon when the *Sea Nymph* entered the Penobscot Bay to pass between the familiar Isle au Haut and Deer Island. When the ship cast anchor in the harbor, people began to pour from the buildings to gather on the shore, cheering. Some took to their boats to row out to the ship. It was Christmas Eve.

"There is enough food and oil for all. Go back to the shore and wait for our boats to come," Stroud ordered. Then turning to his first mate, he said, "See to it, and have a boat filled with supplies lowered for Captain Jarden and me to go ashore."

Matthew Jarden's heart was beating fast as he and Captain Stroud strode up the hill toward his home, with arms laden with parcels. He had looked for Rosa's face in the crowd, but she was not there.

He took the lead around to the side door, noting all the draperies had been pulled. The door was locked, and at his knock he heard the scraping of a chair. The door was opened a crack as two black eyes peered out at him. Then Cally recognized him and swung the door open wide.

"Cap'n! Oh Cap'n, yo' home!"

"Where's Rosa, Cally?"

"Missy Rosa in her room with Miss Martha. I get."

"No, Cally—*I* get," he laughed joyously, unloading the parcels into her arms, heading down the hall to rap loudly on her door.

"What is it, Cally? You don't have to knock the door down!" Rosa scolded sweetly, swinging the door open.

Her expression changed to one of sheer joy, and she rushed into his arms. "Father! Oh, Father, you *did* make it home for Christmas," she cried. "I knew you would! I've been praying every day you would come back to me, and you did!" She leaned back to look up at him. "But you're so thin! Oh, Father—what has happened to you?"

"It's a long story, Rosa; come, I want you to meet the man who saved my life," he said, leading her to where Captain Stroud waited.

Christmas Day dawned with a light snow falling. A sound overhead awakened Rosa with a start. Though the men had talked long into the night, her father was already up and moving about in his room. She thought of the many memories that must have come back to haunt him. Poor man! Little wonder he was disturbed. He was surrounded by all her mother's things, still as she had left them. Besides, Christmas had always been Elizabeth Jarden's favorite time of the year.

Christmas! Christmas Day! Her wedding day! A new beginning!

"Oh, Father, if only you could be as happy as I," she whispered softly.

Over breakfast, her father was in a cheerful mood, even teasing Martha. Midmorning he took Charger out for a ride, coming in at noon with John. Both men had a mysterious air about them, but only Cally took notice.

That afternoon, in the sitting room decorated with green garlands and red ribbons, Rosa Surgosa Jarden became Mrs. John Giles. Captain Stroud led them in their vows, with her father, Cally, Shonto, and Martha looking on. After the ceremony, her father had an announcement to make.

"I have met a wonderful woman in Boston and have asked her to be my wife. Since I will be making my home there for the present, this home is to be for John and Rosa and for all of you for as long as you wish."

During the merriment afterward, Rosa slipped away to her room. It was there Cally found her on her knees. Rosa lifted a happy, tear-stained face to Cally's concerned one.

"Oh, Cally—you're right! Our God is a biiig God!"

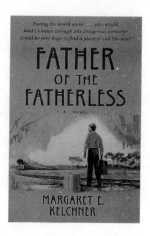

A SHADOW FROM THE HEAT

When Wes Scott leaves his home in Savannah, Georgia, in a desperate search for his wayward sister, Testa, who had run off with a "gamblin' man," little does he realize the long, perilous journey ahead. Deep into the vast reaches of the Southwest desert Testa's abuser flees, dragging her along—with Wes in relentless pursuit. Nearing starvation and without water, Wes comes face-to-face with the bitter reality that he might not survive the cruel elements and many other dangers of the frontier himself—much less save Testa.

Wes must cling to God's promise that He will be "a shadow from the heat." Will that promise be enough?

Can he save his sister and the woman he loves?
Can he save himself?

AT083-411-5158

Purchase from your local bookstore
Or order from
Beacon Hill Press of Kansas City

800-877-0700